MW01137679

MURDER
IN THE SHORES

SUSANNE SIR'S

MURDER
IN THE SHORES
the fortune cookie

Enjoy!

Susanne Sir

2015

TATE PUBLISHING
AND ENTERPRISES, LLC

Published by Tate Publishing & Enterprises, LLC
127 E. Trade Center Terrace | Mustang, Oklahoma 73064 USA
1.888.361.9473 | www.tatepublishing.com

Tate Publishing is committed to excellence in the publishing industry. The company reflects the philosophy established by the founders, based on Psalm 68:11,
"The Lord gave the word and great was the company of those who published it."

Book design copyright © 2014 by Tate Publishing, LLC. All rights reserved.
Cover design by Gian Philipp Rufin
Interior design by Caypeeline Casas

Published in the United States of America

ISBN: 978-1-63185-396-8
1. Fiction / Mystery & Detective / Women Sleuths
2. Fiction / Mystery & Detective / General
14.08.28

A cookie can make a fortune.
A cute cookie can make a fortune.
A fortune can be made from a cookie.

—Author unknown

Dedicated to my husband, who encouraged the creation of this book. My moon and stars.

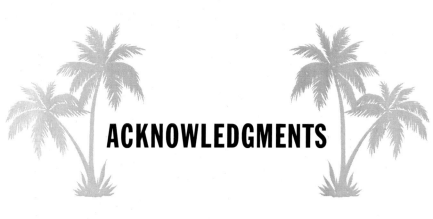

ACKNOWLEDGMENTS

I would like to thank all who contributed to this book. Some of you are unaware of your contribution, and others will be aware of their contribution. To all of you, my thanks for your assistance and your part in creating an entertaining read.

Individual thanks to my book buddies Kimberly Defreitas and Howard Strong.

Gracias to Sid Reese for the use of his book library on the Presbyterian Church and Miami Shores.

Many thanks to Steve Charles for his technical assistance and patience.

My gratitude to Eddie Nunez for his persistence to complete a job with a positive attitude to make it happen.

My thanks to Seth Bramson, the authority for the Florida East Coast Railroad for his encouragement.

Thanks also to Elizabeth Esper, Library Director, and Michelle Brown, Adult Services Librarian of the Brockway Memorial Library.

A special thanks to John Challenor (Phone Doctor) the Great Philanthropist.

Last but not least my Christian publisher—Tate Publishing and their staff—an answer to my prayers.

INTRODUCTION

I drove my 1965 candy-apple red Mustang convertible into my garage. I parked the car and started to walk out of the garage when I looked up and saw what looked like a scarecrow or a ghost tied to the lamppost across the street. It was Halloween time, and it was dark. As I stared at it further, I noticed it was human, and it was not moving!

I am getting ahead of myself. Let me start at the beginning...

CHAPTER 1

I stepped out on my front step and closed the door behind me. I took a deep breath, savoring it, and let my mind acknowledge the blue sky, the white clouds, and the delicious smell to the air. It was October in Florida, and humidity was a thing of the past, but there was one more reason to celebrate. I was looking forward to vacation. Two weeks of vacation and my employer, United Air Lines, had suggested that I should feel free to take even more time.

I know that sounds odd. I have just finished working two years steady without any time off other than occasional days. I flew constantly. If an employee canceled their trip, I was always on the list to fly it. I was in the air more than on the ground. Maybe I was related to Super Women. Then again, I had strawberry-blonde hair, not black. I was five feet five inches tall and in good shape, thanks to my sister's exercise program. No, I am not a pilot. I am a stewardess. Or rather I was, but due to dedication and maybe a little ability, I was promoted to chief stewardess and then also given the title of public relations coordinator. I actually could do both jobs, since publicity recently was rather quiet in Miami.

This two-year work-a-thon was due to my unexpected divorce to Thomas Walters. Neither of us attended the final hearing. What does that tell you? I just couldn't bear to acknowledge my failure. It was too painful. I had come from a happy home and had expected the same. Once I was divorced, I discovered I was pregnant. After a few months I lost the baby. This hit me hard. I needed to take time to reflect on my life and somehow come to terms with two great losses. It seems odd that working yourself to death could help you work out your problems. For me it was just the opposite; when I was up in the friendly skies, I felt less pressure and was able to try and sort out the cause to my problems and find solutions.

I started down the stairs, humming to myself. When I reached the first floor I turned to the right and proceeded down the hall to our community bulletin board. Here I posted the apartment monthly event. It happened to be an animal Halloween costume contest for this coming Saturday at 6:00 p.m. at our Animal Mart Pet Store on Biscayne Boulevard.

My mom and dad had bought the apartment complex I lived in from a Frenchman named Mr. LaPointe in the 1960s. Mr. LaPointe had built the apartments of coral rock in the early 1950s on a triangular piece of property on

Northeast 6th Avenue in Miami Shores. Miami Shores is a quaint village. It is north of Miami and is on the bay. He had named the building LaPointe, naturally, after himself. The front entrance also sat on one of the points of the triangle. My mom and dad are no longer alive. Dad passed of Parkinson's disease, and my mom of heartbreak shortly after his death. This left my sister, Borg's, and me as owners. Our last name is Muldahl. Yes, we are Norwegian. We also inherited trust funds.

I turned as I heard my name called. "Inga!"

It was my best friend Gina's mom, who we fondly referred to as Mama Rosa. This was due to her petite size. She was Italian and moved her arms when speaking or yelling, as could be the case for Gina or me, with lots of speed and grace. I often thought of her arms as propellers. Gina and her mom shared a two-bedroom on the first floor. Gina's dad had passed away after an accident. He had worked for the city of Miami Dade Metro Bus System as a dispatcher and had left them with a nice pension.

Mama Rosa rushed up and gave me a hug. She wished me a happy vacation, and after the formalities were over, she then told me that her toilets and sinks were backing up. I returned her hug and said I would get her a plumber today.

Back on the third floor, also known as the Penthouse, since it was on the top floor, I called Borgs to see if she had our plumber's phone number.

"He moved away," she said. She then told me to wait as she pulled out the yellow pages.

This is rather embarrassing. Does anyone use these? Maybe a minority, but then which one? Miami has so many minorities. Borgs is twenty years older than me, and if she feels comfortable with this, than it is okay with me.

She gave me four different listings, and before she hung up she asked if I could take Annie, her Cocker Spaniel, for a haircut at the dog parlor. Borgs stated that Greta, her goose, might also want to come for the ride. I know that sounds odd, and it is but you will develop a better understanding as we continue.

Borgs is a widow. Her hair is a pale blonde, and her eyes are blue, the same color as mine. Only mine change to green depending on what I am wearing. She is slim, teaches aerocise at the Miami Shores Community Center, and is attractive. I am partial; after all, she is my sister.

She stated she needed to get supplies for our restaurant, the Pie, before they opened, but I'll tell you more about that later. She gave me the time of Annie's appointment, and I hung up.

I dialed the first number, a man answered quickly and yelled, "Plumber!"

Good, we were moving along. Little did I know that he answered that way because he did not know much English?

I explained the problem, and he said, "Si."

I naturally then assumed he was Spanish, most likely Cuban because of the Miami connection. I proceeded with, "Senor, what time will you be here?"

"Whata senor? I ama Frank." I heard in return.

I then took a deep breath. I guessed he was not Spanish and just said, "What time?"

"Si, 1:00 p.m." Frank said.

Good, we could move forward. I then said, "Do you know the LaPointe?"

"Si, plumbing problem."

"No," I said. "The location is the LaPointe."

"Si, thata is whata I need."

"Good, LaPointe."

"Si, please."

I felt a need to terminate this conversation and did so; all I needed was to get my point across. I then dialed the second number Borgs had given me.

This one answered right away with, "Plumber!"

I thought they must all answer this way, quick and to the point. I then told him what the problem was.

"Si."

"What did you just say?" I asked.

"Si."

"Do you know where the LaPointe is?" I then said.

"Si, I knowa the pointa." Then he hung up.

Okay, onward to the third phone number. Good thing I had more than one.

This time when the phone was picked up, I did not hear, "Plumber!" I heard, "The point if you please?" but in a young girl's voice. She sounded so sweet I immediately calmed down.

"My name is Maria Jade. Please excuse my father. He is Italian and does not speak much English, but he is a good plumber," she said.

I gave the address, and she said he would be there shortly. After all, if he was a good plumber, that is the point!

I updated Mama Rosa that Frank would be arriving shortly. Maybe he just always says 1:00 p.m. It would be interesting to see how Frank got along with Mama Rosa! Si.

CHAPTER 2

My cell phone started to sing "Blue Skies," and I picked up the call to hear Babes wish me a happy vacation. Babes also had an apartment at the Pointe, which she shares with the Crane. They both attend Barry University and hold down part-time jobs for extra money. They have assistance from their parents for university costs, apartment rent, and food. Crane was lucky enough to have won a girls' basketball scholarship. So goes the nickname for Crane, who is not only tall but a cute Midwestern with blonde hair and freckles across her nose.

Now Babes has dyed her hair a bright pink, and she is well endowed up front. She has dimples on either side of her mouth. She resembles the front of a DC8 jet scoops. She definitely stands out in a crowd.

Babes asked if I would go with her to the dentist tomorrow.

"Yes, and how about taking a ride with me around 2:00 p.m.?" I asked.

She was game.

I decided to gas up my car at the Shores Chevron and then swing by and pick up Babes. I went downstairs and opened the only garage door in the apartment. There sat one of the loves of my life—a 1965 candy-apple red Mustang convertible with a white top. The interior was red. You can imagine the maintenance on this beauty of a vintage car. I would not have been able to manage if it had not been for the young mechanic, JR, at Miami Shores Auto Repair Shop on Northeast 2nd Avenue. He was a genius.

I backed the car out and put down the top. I put the pedal to the medal. Nothing like living it up. Life is good, or rather life was good until I heard a siren and saw a flashing light in my rear mirror. Hoping it was not for me, I pulled over, and so did the police car. Sadly, it was for me.

I was getting my license and registration out when I heard a familiar voice. "Hi, Inga."

Maybe there was some hope here. It was Chief Walters, my ex's Brother Bob. Both the Walter boys had attended and graduated Fordham. Tom decided to go into detective work and hi-tech security by opening his own business, while Bob obviously went into police work. Their dad was a judge in Miami. So it seems they had all bases covered. Both men were over six feet. Bob was a little taller than Tom. Tom's hair was a lighter shade of blond. They both had blue eyes and worked out. What a combination: money and good looks.

I batted my eyes and adjusted my smile to cute. With an innocent look on my face, I said, "Chief, since when do you work street patrol, or was this just a friendly stop?"

"Well, Inga, a little of both. Do you know how fast you were going? Maybe when you are having so much fun it is hard to keep track of silly things like that."

"You are so right, chief." Now that definitely was another mistake, since he then reached for his citation book and started to write.

He stopped, pen in hand, and said, "It is really good to see you, Inga. How long has it been? Are you free for dinner tonight?"

"Would that mean I do not get a ticket?"

"Now, Inga, what type of example would I be if I did not enforce the law? By the way, I was only writing you a warning."

"Well, if that is the case, I appreciate the offer of diner, but how about trying the new Chinese restaurant over on West Dixie Highway across from Slims? I could go for a cup of soup. Sorry, I cannot make diner."

I received my warning, and we met at the Fortune Cookie.

There were only a few customers sitting at tables so service was fast. We both ordered soup, and while we waited we chatted about old times.

Bob said, "I will always ask you out in hopes I will wear you down one of these days and you will say yes. I also know how strongly you and my brother felt about each other. You looked great together. Inga, he knows you lost the baby. That is when he decided he needed to go to Europe to gain more experience detecting and to educate himself on their equipment. He has been there for two years. Seems like a long time to me."

He then looked up at me and saw tears running down my cheeks. Just as he was handing me his hanky, I noticed a customer who had just walked in pick up a fortune cookie from the table by the cash register and insert a piece of paper into the cookie. He then handed it to the cashier and said he would pick it up later. Bob saw me staring at them, and the next thing I know our table is upended and my soup is in my lap.

Bob jumped up and started blotting me and the table as the waiter rushed over to help.

He looked at me and said, "I need to apologize to you twice. Please," he said to the waiter, "get our check and give the lady a soup to go."

Bob walked me to the car, soup in hand. "Before you go, I want you to know that Tom will be home shortly."

"Bob, thanks for the soup and the second warning notice you gave me today." I squeezed his hand. "I appreciate the invitation. Didn't that look suspicious with that customer handing the fortune cookie to the cashier after he had put something in it?"

He tousled my hair and said, "I don't want you to think of anything suspicious or get involved. Just leave that up to me."

I left Bob to head home for a change of clothes and to call Babes with an update of when we were leaving. I thought again of what I had seen in the Chinese restaurant and how I needed to look into this further. It stirred my curiosity. I thought of Tom coming home. I then turned up the music, watched my speed limit, and put a smile on my face.

CHAPTER 3

As I was walking out of my apartment I then heard, "Ripper." Ripper is a boy baby parrot, the little man of the house.

"Ripper, I guess you want to go for a ride too and see your cousins," I said.

I walked over to his cage. He went to the bathroom quickly. Ripper is a gentle parrot and would not go to the bathroom on me. Smart little guy. He jumped on my finger, hopped onto my shoulder, and moved to the back of my neck. This was one of his favorite positions. I think he hoped that I would forget he was there and he could just stay with me. I was wearing a wide brim straw hat with ladybugs and sunflowers on it. Ripper was well hidden. Maybe he was a little spy guy.

I met Babes downstairs, and we got into my car. We headed to Borg's house. I was also watching the speed limit. Borgs has a combination lock on her front door. So I put in the code and was greeted by Annie. There was something familiar about Annie, other than looking like a Cocker Spaniel.

Annie has blonde hair with a lot of red in it, a little darker in color than my hair. Here is the funny part. She was wearing a wide-brimmed sunbonnet exactly like mine. Had to be Borgs's weird sense of humor. I could picture her laughing when she put the bonnet on Annie. She had to have made it and waited for the perfect time.

I looked down at Annie, who looked up, so cute. "Okay, Annie, anyone can tell we are related," I said.

Babes, had her phone out taking a picture, muttering, "My mom won't believe this."

I could understand that, since I was in wonder also. It was then that I heard Greta quack.

Borgs lives on a lake in Miami Shores, Marina Lake. It was spring fed so you could swim, boat without an engine, or fish.

Babes, Annie, and I headed out the back door, and to further my pleasure, Greta the goose was wearing bunny ears. Babes was now doubled over laughing and adding more pictures to send to her mom. Soon her mom would be calling me to cancel her lease.

I approached Greta, saying, "If you want to take a ride you need to take off the bunny ears."

Greta smartly sidestepped me. I countered, and she re countered. I started toward her, saying I had a treat for her, but this goose had an attitude. As I got close Greta spread her wings and took to flight. I could not counter that. She headed right for my car and landed on my backseat, bunny ears still in place. I got my blanket out of the trunk and placed it across the backseat. I then got my phone out and dialed Borgs. She answered laughing.

"What is Greta doing with bunny ears?" was my first remark.

It was a simple question, and simple was the answer.

"She likes them and will not take them off. Maybe she thinks it gives her height." More giggles and Babes has totally lost it now.

"How did you know I would be wearing my sun hat?" my second remark.

"The weather. On a serious note, could you swing by the Pie later? I would like to roll out our incentive GD program for the employees," Borgs said.

GD stood for good deed. Borgs and I had started this amongst ourselves in memory of her late husband, Tully, who had died when doing a good deed. He was standing on the curb of Northeast 2nd Avenue waiting for the light to change when he saw a dog dart across the street. Tully's heart was as big as gold for everyone, but especially animals dependent on humans for care and safety. He rushed after the dog and pushed it away in time, but not enough time for him to get out of the motorist's way. The dog took off.

The heavens had been good to Tully and us. They had left him earthbound as a ghost to look over the animals, like an animal angel. Well, Borgs and I decided we would have a GD contest once a month between each other, competing for the best good deed. Whomever was the winner took the other to the restaurant of their choice.

"Talking of this Borgs, the other day I saw an elderly women pulling a wheel cart loaded with groceries struggling down Northeast 6th Avenue just coming from Publix. I stopped and loaded the groceries in my car and drove her home. Then helped her in her house with the bags." I finished

"I am surprised she got in the car with you. Didn't she know better?" Borgs said.

"Well," I said, "She did kind of know me. It was your next-door neighbor."

"That doesn't count!" Borgs yelled.

"Well, what did you do for GD?" I yelled.

"Me, I just made you laugh today." Borgs giggled.

"That doesn't count either."

"What if I stop over the Pie after I drop Annie off at the dog parlor? Do you mind if I bring Babes?"

"Fine, bring Babes, but take your time. I am still picking up the supplies that they needed."

I turned and asked Babes if she was free.

"Are you kidding? I can't wait to go to the Pie."

If there is anything Babes loves other than bubble gum, it is sweets and pizza pie. Everything settled, we all got in the car. Annie and Greta were in the backseat, and Babes and I were in front. Babes started to chew on some of her favorite bubble gum and was shortly blowing huge bubbles.

We were only a short distance from the dog parlor. The dog parlor was just off the main drag in the Shores. Driving along, I heard a strange noise behind us. Like car brakes squealing and then a crash. I wasn't too concerned, since I again was watching the speed limit. It was when I heard the siren and then the now-familiar flashing light in my rearview mirror that I got concerned.

I thought, *Is this what vacation is like?*

I also pulled over. Things now went straight downhill. I looked over at Babes, who was hidden by a huge bubble. The officer approached the driver's side, and I realized it was not the chief but someone I had never seen before.

His opening statement was, "Look what you did." He pointed down the street to a car that was up on the sidewalk with its hood facing into a telephone poll.

"Officer"—I checked his badge—"Mendez, I did not hit them," I answered.

"You didn't have to hit them. You were such a distraction here on Main Street that they lost control of their car," he roughly stated.

"What distraction?" I said in defense of myself. It again was not the best thing to say.

Officer Mendez proceeded to then scream at me. "What distraction? What is that duck wearing bunny ears for?

Then you and the dog have matching bonnets. Who is this in the front seat with you, Bobblehead?"

He then started to walk around to the passenger side to, I guess, get a better look at "Bobblehead."

"I want you to know, Officer Mendez that is not a duck. Greta is a goose. The dog is related to me."

The officer had also managed to get Ripper mad. Ripper started to prance back and forth on the back of my neck and then let out a blood-curdling scream. I could read my little man's mind. *You don't treat my mommy like that, or the trouble has only just begun.* No truer scream was uttered.

Just then my cell went off. I excused myself and answered. It was Gina on the other end. She is the dispatcher for the Shores Police.

"I will speak fast. I just got a call that there was a spotting of Noah's Ark going down on 2nd Avenue. I knew it must be you."

Really!

She continued with, "I put a call into the chief. He will be there shortly."

As I put my cell away, I noticed Officer Mendez had an expression of fear on his face. Way to go, Ripper. After Ripper's scream, Annie started to bark, and Greta was honking. Then passing cars started to hit their horns. The cars were now bumper-to-bumper and not moving.

I saw a driver almost across from me roll down his window and start yelling at the car in front of him to "Move it,

Turtle Head." He was ignored. I could see the driver's face getting red with anger.

There was more honking from the cars and Greta. Then Red Face opened his door and hustled over to the car in front.

Turtle Head rolled down his window and said, "You need to take a pill for that hot flash," and quickly rolled up his window. Just in time.

I could see Red Face curling his fingers into a fist and starting to flash his fist in front of Turtle Head's face. This seemed to be the last straw for Turtle Head. Turtle Head opened his door and started to get out of his car just as Red Face took a swing at him, which he blocked. Turtle Head continued to unravel from the car to his full height as he grew to Giant Turtle Head.

As he came out of the car he also took a swing at Red Face and flattened him to the ground. Cheers sounded from all around. The barking and honking continued as Giant Turtle Head and Red Face glared at each other. Of course, Red Face was glaring from the ground up.

Down the street there was a young girl walking a dog that seemed to be the size of a small pony. I guess the barking set him off, and he started with a bound toward the action, dragging the young girl, who somehow was able to hang onto his collar and bring herself up unto his back. They were now in a full gallop in the middle of Main Street and headed our way.

As Pony Dog approached Red Face on the ground, Pony Dog rose in the air gracefully with his rider intact and cleared the body of Red Face. Pony Dog came to a graceful stop next to our car.

I looked at the young girl, who was now dismounting Pony Dog. I said, "That was quite a walk-ride jump you just did. Do you ride horses? I asked.

"No this is my first experience with Bear," she answered. "We just got him. He was a police dog but was too big to get into small places for sniffing. My name is Kelly. I have never seen so much excitement in the Shores."

I thought to myself, *I haven't either, and I wish I was not at the center of it.*

Just then I noticed Annie looking sexy, peeking out from under the brim of her hat with a sidelong glance at Bear. Oh dear! Bear had zoned in on Annie and was drooling all over me with his tongue hanging out and panting.

Officer Mendez had just reached Bobblehead's door, or rather Babes. He was standing in front of the passenger door handle, and I tried to tell him that was not a good idea. But it was too late. Babes went into action and hit the door handle and swung it fast and wide. Officer Mendez almost disappeared below the door. Just in the nick of time Chief Walters showed up, or so I hoped.

"Officer Mendez," the chief said. "For your first day you seem to be right on top of things, or should I say under them."

A grunt sounded.

"Maybe you would like to return to the station and take a break. I'll handle this for you."

Officer Mendez was in a crouched position and was trying to waddle away when another officer pulled around the corner and loaded him into the squad car.

Chief Walters was now taking pictures of my car. He was wearing a big grin. I reached into my purse and put on a big pair of sunglasses. The better for anyone not to see me with my dear. I glanced over at Babes, and she was still hidden behind the bubble, but her shoulders were shaking. I am sure with laughter. She could at least come out of hiding and help me face the music.

I than noticed people waving from the Shores Library across the street. Oh no, there was the twins Jay and Steve Burner, who also lived at the apartment complex. They were working at the library and sometimes confused people by dressing alike and causing mass chaos by switching places with each other. If one was given an order, the other would step in and not complete the request. Then when questioned about the completion, he would say he knew nothing about the order, which of course he did not. They both had majors in English. They were tall, good-looking, and very funny. They now stood tall with cameras in hand, busily taking pictures of Noah's ark and knowing exactly what they were doing. The little devils.

My concern was for the car up on the curb. As I looked back, I noticed another patrol car with them. I asked Chief Walter about it.

I expected some more screaming, but his comment was, "He will be lucky we don't ticket him for careless driving. He did not hit the light pole, only jumped the curb."

Several more patrol cars arrived and started to disperse traffic. I waved good-bye to Kelly and Bear. What a relief.

"Well, I guess I can go, then?"

"Thanks for these great pictures. Inga, you told me you are on vacation?" the Chief said.

"Yes."

"How long have you been on vacation?"

"This is the first day."

"How long is your vacation?"

"Two weeks."

"I need to get back to the station and post overtime. Later."

No later for me. I had enough of flashing lights and sirens!

CHAPTER 4

I put the car in gear again, watching the speed limit, and headed off. I glanced over at my passenger, who had now removed her camouflage and had decided to chew the gum instead. In record time we pulled up in front of the dog parlor.

I came around to Annie's side and said, "It is time to get the latest gossip from the dog parlor."

Annie did not move. Did I mention Annie has selective hearing? Evidently she was deciding not to hear this command, since it was more exciting riding in the car with Aunt Inga. I decided to entice the offer by saying there was a treat inside. This got Greta moving. She got behind Annie and pushed. They both spilled out of the backseat.

I then told Greta to get back in the car, but the goose with the attitude was waddling right behind Annie into the shop. I turned over Annie to the groomer and was about to leave when I saw Greta headed for the treat dish.

I got between the dish and Greta, and trying to distract the groomer, by asking when Annie would be ready.

"A couple of hours," was my answer.

As I nodded my head, I quickly scooped up a treat for Greta, only to hear from behind my neck, "Ripper."

Not batting an eye, I picked up another treat and then headed for the door. The groomer was looking at my hand and shaking her head. What we do for our kids. I must remember to tell Borgs to leave an extra tip.

We headed back to Borgs's house to drop off Greta. She was the perfect goose. She marched right to the back yard and waited for her treat. I knew she did this just so I would not remember her behavior for next time. Onward to my apartment. I gave Ripper a kiss and his treat. He was in charge. As I was leaving I saw the flashing light on my answering machine. I pushed the button, and it was Gina again.

"I have told everyone we are not friends anymore and I will never see you. Now the hard part. There is a baby shower tomorrow night for Captain Colson and his wife. You have been invited. You need to pick up a present from both of us. Baby N U. Later." What loyalty.

Finally we are now pulling up in front of the Pie on Northeast 6th Avenue. The Pie is open only four days a week. We serve real homemade pie and coffee or tea in the afternoons on little tables for two and then serve pizza pie from 5:00 p.m. until closing, which would be 10:00 to11:00

p.m. The staff are all retirees. Borgs had gotten the idea to post the job listing at the Shores Community Center.

Our chef, referred to as Cook, was a retired mess cook from the navy. We sent him to Johnson and Whales to learn how to do all the tricks. It was a dream come true for him, and believe me, these pies are to die for.

Our deliveryman is an ex-cab driver and knew every street in the area. He is called Cabby. He drives a smart car with a chef strapped to the top with a pizza pie in one hand and a mile high pie in the other. I worried that it may cause the car to turn over, but he said it was no problem.

Our waitress is a mom whose kids grew up. She is called Hon. Our cashier and hostess is an ex accountant named Numbers. It was their idea with the names. Borgs is called Chief, and I am Skipper. We are all huddled around a large table for our meeting.

Everyone had a slice of pie. Babes had two. She couldn't decide. Borgs proceeded to explain our incentive plan. They liked the idea of doing a good deed and competing for the top place. The winner would receive a hundred dollars. We would keep a board in the kitchen with all the good deeds and once a month vote on them.

The employees then brought up their concerns and suggestions. I brought up the new Chinese restaurant. Always worried about our competition. I asked Cabby if he noticed that they had a lot of deliveries.

"I'll keep my eyes open and let you know."

Borgs excused herself to pick up Annie and stated she would return after dropping her at home. I reminded her to leave a nice tip. Babes announced she needed to get to work and also study later. Babes is a waitress at Slims. She called Crane and asked if she would pick her up on the way to basketball practice. She agreed for a piece of pie.

Crane drove a used Beetle, affectionately called LB (short for Ladybug). Yes, it was painted red with black dots all over it. Her only complaint was getting in and out of the little car. I taught her the evacuation process in planes for going out windows. This is working perfect for her.

When Borgs returned she said that there was a huge black dog almost the size of a pony sitting in front of the dog parlor. It tried to go in with her. The owner opened the door just a tiny bit and grabbed her arm, pulling her inside without the dog. The owner explaining that shortly after Annie arrived, so did the Pony Dog. As they were looking out the window, a young girl showed up with a leash. Once Pony Dog was secured, he left with the young girl. How do I explain Pony Dog Bear has a crush on Annie to Borgs? Sometimes it is best not to speak.

Borgs and I hung out at the Pie, helping and getting in the way. Everyone loved having us and tried to keep us out of too much trouble. We all worked on our cleaning projects. Borgs kept complaining I was eating all the profits and I would need to spend the next month working off all the extra pounds I had put on in one night. It is hard to keep the pounds off when you start to age, so the employees enjoyed hearing someone else get scolded.

I called Gina back to confirm the baby shower invitation. I asked her how the plumber worked out.

"Fine, he is putting in a sprinkler system on Saturday for Mom's orchard plants." Gina said.

"You are kidding."

"Si."

Frank seems to be making quite an impression.

I headed home. As I was stopping at a light, I noticed the person in the car next to me was dressed all in black. He also had a black face and drove a black car. Now how nondescript is that? His only distinguishing features were the white of his eyes and his teeth. If he closed his eyes and shut his mouth, he would be a shadow. He got my attention. Upon further scrutiny, I recognized him as an employee of Tom's security company.

I think my name should have been George, or more definitive Georgi, as in curious and female. So I naturally followed him. Guess where he pulled in?

You guessed it. The Fortune Cookie. He parked at a distance from the restaurant and in the shadows. Then he turned off his lights. This was appearing to be an all-nighter, so I continued on home, watching my speed limit.

Exhausted and full of food, when I got home that night I hit the bed and was fast asleep in no time.

I dreamed of fortune cookies and secret messages.

CHAPTER 5

The next morning upon waking up, enjoying a cup of coffee and a shower, I called Borgs.

"Good morning, sis. You made me feel so guilty last night concerning my over consumption of food that I have decided to turn over a new leaf and go for a bike ride at Uleta State Park this morning. Would you like to come?"

Borgs's answer was to inform me she was holding an exercise class at the community center at 9:00 a.m., saying I should join her there.

"Is Betty going to be there?" I asked

Betty is Miss Perfect. At least that is *her* opinion. My answer was yes.

"Okay, I will meet you there. There is a baby shower tonight at the police station for Captain Colson and his wife. I need to get a present from Gina and myself. Would you like to help me pick out a baby present at Baby N U after our workout? You could come with us tonight."

"I would will love to help pick out the present. Babies are such fun. I will need to pass on the shower this evening. Later," Borgs answered.

I rushed into the bedroom to get into my workout clothes that matched! I fixed my hair into a cute ponytail. Betty wouldn't be the only well-dressed participant. I then headed for the center.

Borgs quickly had the class moving at a fast pass. I noticed Betty seemed sluggish. She also looked like she had gained some weight. This made me smile and work a little harder. I know that sounds childish, but you don't know Miss Perfect. Gina, Betty, and I were in the same homeroom in high school. Everything she did had to be perfect. Her homework was free of any food stains, and never was a sheet of paper bent or crumbled. All her outfits were color coordinated. She did whatever it took to steal our boyfriends, sometimes succeeding, and that is why she is so hated.

After class I tried to make small talk with Betty while waiting for Borgs to say good-bye to everyone, but Betty just kind of slunk away with her head down. Borgs was watching Betty and said she wasn't herself lately.

Borgs and I took showers and changed at the center. We got into my car and headed for Baby N U.

As soon as we entered the store, we noticed this grandmother with a twin girl and boy on what looked like a leash. The children had red hair and wore glasses. We just couldn't help ourselves and stopped the grandmother to remark on how cute the twins were.

"These kids are a menace," Grandma remarked.

Both Borgs and I looked at each other. That was an odd thing to say, we thought.

The grandmother proceeded to tell us the boy was Dennis and the girl was Denise Menace.

Borgs and I looked at each other and smiled in agreement; now the comment made sense.

She then told us that when the twins were born they both had colic and cried for a year and a half. She said that neither her daughter nor she slept in that time. As the twins got older, no one had enough energy to discipline them.

Borgs and I looked at each other again. I thought, *That is an odd thing to say for a grandmother.*

"Stay clear of them. I warned you!" Grandma said waving her finger at us.

We moved quickly away from Sergeant Grandma. The bassinette section was ahead of us, and we darted into the department. I mentioned to Borgs that since Gina and I were sharing the cost we could get a bigger gift. Borgs's eyes lit up, and she headed in the direction of her stare.

I followed, and when I saw what she was headed for, I agreed it was definitely the perfect present. It was white and all lace, bows, and ruffles. We wrote down the number and decided to pick up a few more items to place into the bassinette before checking out. That is when we heard the scream.

We were just walking into the main aisle when a stroller went by at top speed. The little guy in it had short black curls, and his arms were up in the air. He was yelling, "Weeeeeeeee!"

We looked in the direction the stroller had come and saw Dennis Menace overlooking his handy work with a big smile on his face. He was also loose. No Sergeant Grandma. We stepped back as a bigger version of the baby in the stroller, also with short black curls, came running and screaming down the aisle with a look of horror on her face. Her arms were up in the air too. Must be mom. We walked up to Master Menace and asked were his grand-mother was. Dennis took out a peashooter and shot both of us in the neck.

It was then that sales clerk Miss Pinacle (I read her name plate) arrived. She had a rather pinched face, which I figured was from the really tight bun she wore at her neck. It gave her an instant face-lift. Unfortunately it also enlarged her nostrils and slanted her eyes. I thought she looked a little like Miss Piggy and figured the kids would probably like the look.

When she spoke I noticed it was hard for her to move her lips, but she did get out the words in a snarl, "Get hold of your child!"

That only made Dennis laugh harder. As I opened my mouth to protest, I got a spitball flying into it. I didn't linger; I needed to escape. I grabbed Borgs's hand and ran toward cover. As I rounded the corner of the diaper section, I saw Denise Menace on the floor with a stack of diapers. She must have used her teeth to open the package.

Denise had unfolded all the diapers, and in the center of the diaper she was placing a spoonful of carrots from a baby food jar. She must have come prepared with lunch. Just then Miss Piggy rounded the corner and stepped on the diaper and into the carrots.

Denise then started to yell, "Kaka!" and point at Miss Piggy.

Miss Piggy looked down with disgust on her face, saying, "Kaka?"

To add to the fun, Dennis arrived and shot Miss Piggy in the rear with his peashooter. The security guard showed up, following Dennis with his hand on his gun and his mouth open. Denise shot a spoonful of carrots into his open mouth.

After a moment we heard "Mmmmm. That is delicious."

"You are disgusting! You are a pig!" Miss Piggy ran over to the guard yelling.

"Look who is calling who a pig!"

Thank God Sergeant Grandma appeared. She pushed Miss Piggy aside, not too gently, to see who was yelling, "Kaka pig." Grandma got her leashes out and snapped in place on Dennis and Denise before you could say "kaka." We left Miss Piggy to handle her own problems.

Grandma headed toward the front door with both the Menaces in tow. Looking back at us, she said, "I warned you." She was also shaking her finger at us, again. Maybe this helped her stress level.

I thought to myself, *No one could have warned us enough for this disaster.*

Borgs and I headed to the check-out lane and collected our purchases. Somehow I had picked up a miniature Miss Piggy to go in the bassinette; after all, it was quite a momentous morning. We loaded the bassinette into the rear seat of my car. As we were leaving Baby N U, the Adventura Police were pulling in. I hope they didn't know Chief Walters.

I pulled away slowly, watching my speed limit, and headed home.

CHAPTER 6

I drove into my garage after dropping Borgs off and closed the garage door, leaving the bassinette in the back seat, along with mini Miss Piggy. I called Babes as I was headed to my apartment and asked if we could take her scooter to the dentist.

"That is fine," Babes said, "as long as you drive."

I asked about grabbing something to eat first.

"What a great idea. I may not be able to eat later," she answered.

"Meet me in five minutes downstairs," I said.

As we later saw each other, we both started to laugh. Oddly, we were both dressed all in pink. Babe's scooter was also pink, and we had two matching pink helmets.

Babes wanted to know where we were going for lunch, and I answered, "It is a surprise." A surprise for her but not for me. Fortune Cookie here we come.

We headed down Northeast 6th Avenue. We were a vision in pink with Babes blowing bubbles with her pink gum. I must be hearing sirens and flashing lights in my sleep. No, there was a patrol car behind me. I now naturally automatically pulled over.

Chief Walters approached. I noticed Officer Mendez riding shotgun. Babes was in hiding behind another pink bubble.

Chief's opening comment was, "Trying to confuse us with different transportation?"

"No, of course not. We are really the top of a wedding cake and are in the process of delivering it. By the way, I don't think we were speeding, so why are we being stopped?" I answered and asked.

"I just wanted to share with you that the Adventura Police Chief called to ask if I knew anyone who owned a candy-apple red Mustang convertible 1965. They are thinking of banning this person from the Baby N U store due to a small riot," Chief Walters stated.

I gulped and questioned the answer he gave.

"I switched the conversation to the Dolphins upcoming game against the Patriots"—the Adventura Chief was from Boston—"and we made a bet against each other and the honor of both of our cities. I then said I needed to hang up and never answered the question."

"Bob, how can I ever thank you?"

He answered with, "I said, I had to apologize to you twice yesterday. Once for making you cry and once for spilling soup in your lap. Consider this apology one. I gather that you are planning to attend the baby shower for Captain Colson and his wife tonight?"

My answer was yes.

Chief was not finished yet. "And how will we be entertaining ourselves and the Shores Police this afternoon? I just like to be forewarned."

"Actually," I stated, "Babes and I will be at the dentist's office."

Chief Walters nodded his head and said, "My condolences to the dentist."

Well, of all the nerve!

We pulled into the parking lot, and Babes had finally put her balloon blowing aside and stated, "Are we going to Slims?"

"No, cookie, we are going to the Fortune Cookie," I told her.

"Neat."

Once seated, the waiter took our order. That was chop suey. Since we looked alike, we might as well order alike. I was not really interested in the food but wanted to observe what was happening in the restaurant. I was here yesterday with Bob, and he tried to pretend that there was nothing wrong going on. I know he intentionally knocked the table over, spilling the soup to distract me, but I was not fooled. He is not a clumsy person. Second, I had seen the shadow last night working surveillance.

Our food arrived shortly, and there was a lot of it. I then realized I was starved, and looking at Babes, saw she was also. She looked like a chipmunk storing food for the winter. I guess all that bubble blowing helps the cheek muscles.

Once we had eaten everything in sight, I was able to do my own surveillance. I had positioned myself facing the cash register when we were seated. I was limited in what I could do but was watching the front counter and cashier with its big dish of fortune cookies. I was not disappointed.

Within a few minutes in walks Betty Perfect and approaches the front counter, immediately grabbing a cookie. She places a slip of paper into the cookie and leaves saying, "Later." She did not see me, or if she did she choose not to say hi.

Each of us also grabbed a fortune cookie. Babes read her message that she was in for a scare. Mine said to beware of dark halls. I told Babes we needed to pay up and make a pit stop at home. She was in agreement. I left her saying I would be down in thirty minutes.

"Take all the time you want. I am in no hurry to see the dentist," she said.

I ran upstairs, or rather quickly walked, and called Borgs. My first words were, "Are you at the Pie?"

"Yes. You can't be hungry again. A stomach can only hold so much food," my sister said.

"Borgs, did Cabby say anything to you about observing the Fortune Cookie drivers?"

Answering she said, "Now that you bring it up, he did. He said they had a busy night, and he remarked that it seemed odd that business was so good since they had just opened. He was not delivering our pies, since we were not open, but was riding around on his bike for exercise and saw their delivery van often go by him."

I told Borgs I was in a hurry and had to go but not before she gave me a warning to "stay out of trouble and forget the Fortune Cookie."

How could I forget? It was not my nature; after all, I could have been named Georgi.

As I went to lock up, I again heard, "Ripper" spoken.

Turning I said, "I guess you have been cooped up a lot lately. You can come."

Ripper quickly took a bathroom break and jumped on my finger.

"Ripper, I don't have a helmet for you, so get under my hair and move around my neck to the back of my head. We are only going a short distance. Hang tight," I warned Ripper.

Babes was waiting, and we hoped on the scooter and were off to the dentist.

As we rode along, we sang, "We are off to see the dentist, the wonderful dentist in the Shores."

CHAPTER 7

We parked the scooter, and just before entering the office we read a sign posted on the front door: "Beware. Enter at your own risk." I noticed Babes turn and get ready for flight, but I grabbed her arm and opened the door.

Greeting us at the reception desk was a women dressed in a long white, flowing dress with little wings on her back. She was holding a wand with a star on the end.

I looked at Babes, and we both said in unison, "Is this the dentist's office?"

"You are in the right place," and looking at Babes, she said, "So you are you the patient?"

Babes nodded her head and started to blow bubbles.

"Let me introduce myself. I am the Tooth Fairy." The receptionist said.

Well, I thought, *that explains everything. Really?*

Babes completing the paper work she was given got up and returned it to the Tooth Fairy. She directed us to head to the left and to then turn right following the hall until the end and knock on the door before entering. The doctor was waiting for us. Babes wouldn't let go of me, so I guessed I would not be staying to chat with the Tooth Fairy.

When we rounded the corner, before us was a sight to behold. The sign out front now began to make sense, and even the Tooth Fairy. Maybe. At the entrance of the hall were all sizes of pumpkins and spider webs hanging down from the ceiling with little spiders on them. *The younger patients must like coming here*, I thought.

As we entered, Babes stepped on a mat that let out an eerie sound. Once inside the hall, it was almost entirely dark with the exception of a few spotlights. As we proceeded forward, skeletons were draped around the floor and walls hanging onto chains, and the spider webs got longer and thicker. It was like fighting your way through a jungle. This took almost all our attention until a ghost came flying at us, saying, "Woo!" We both shivered.

Determined that if little kids could do this so could we, we proceeded. I heard Ripper prancing on my shoulders and knew even fearless Ripper was feeling uneasy. Babes stumbled over a head that was rolling freely around the floor and screamed. I didn't blame her. I wanted to scream too, but my mouth was frozen.

To further our pleasure, a headless man shot across the hall with a big sword. We stopped in our tracks to let him pass. I was thinking of telling him that his head was further back, but I wasn't sure how a headless man could hear. Our next treat was Frankenstein, who lunged out at us, and then after hovering for a while, receded.

The worst was next. A cackling witch, and ugly as all get out, grabbed both Babes and me. We both screamed at the top of our lungs. We struggled to get out of her death grip. Babe's bubble caught the witch's hair, and they appeared to be glued together. At the same time Ripper decided to take flight with his own treat. Ripper let out a piercing screech that even macaws didn't make, and it was up, up, and away.

At that moment the doctor choose to open the door. I guess he was wondering what happened to us. Some bedside manner. He was not a reassuring sight. He was dressed as Dracula. Cape and all. He had fangs for teeth, and they were dripping with something red. What do I mean something red? It must have been his last patient.

As he stepped forward he noticed and heard Ripper. "It's a bat!" He then screamed out in horror.

Ripper went after him, zooming around and screeching.

At the other end of the hall I heard the Tooth Fairy yelling, "What is going on here?"

She has nerve. Why is she asking us what is going on? This is their show. Ripper heard her voice and headed out of the operating room and toward her. Babes and I were huddled in a corner shaking and attached to the wicked witch by gum. What an advertisement for Bazooka.

The Tooth Fairy lost her nerve when she saw Ripper headed in her direction at full speed. "It's a flying bat!

Help!" again the Tooth Fairy was yelling. She took off as fast as her legs would carry her. Evidently she could not fly. I did notice she did not have her wand. Possibly that made the difference.

The light then went on in the hall, and Dracula came toward us minus the fangs. He reached out his hand to help us up. It took a little longer for Babes, since we had to un-bubble her from the witch. The hall was a total disaster.

Ripper came cruising in and landed on my shoulder, saying, "Ripper."

I rubbed the top of his head. "My hero."

The doctor introduced himself as Dr. Easel. He hoped we had not been too frightened. He then, in an excited voice, said he had not had so much fun in a long time. It was hard to share his enthusiasm. I wanted to mention our fear, but my mouth was still frozen.

Babes was then put in the dentist's chair. A little cloth was draped around her neck, and she was told to open her mouth while he put on surgical gloves. He instructed her to point to the problem. As she did she looked surprised and said the tooth wasn't there anymore. Checking the witch, I found it in her hair.

Dr. Easel cleaned up her gum gently, gave her a prescription for pain, and announced that there would be no charge. He again apologized for frightening us but pointed out that we had also frightened him and the fairy, which was true. He handed both of us his card and encouraged us to call him. We both accepted. Without the fangs he was tall, dark, and good-looking. Maybe he wanted to take us on a date to ride that scary roller coaster in Dania.

We then proceeded to leave, and passing the Tooth Fairy, she said she wanted to offer us another dentist just in case we hesitated in returning and needed help with our teeth. She said he was very up on all the latest procedures and medical equipment and was very patient orientated. He has an office in the 999 building.

We looked at the card she gave us, and it read Dr. G. Cheng. We thanked her and said we now knew why she was the Tooth Fairy. She then smiled and offered us some Halloween candy. Ripper stepped forward and got a raisin.

Babes and I headed back home. I noticed a patrol car following at a slow pace. I also was watching the speed limit and driving at a slow pace.

Once we arrived at the Pointe, I told Babes I needed to rest up after our adventure for the party that night. Babes said she was going to take some medicine and a quick nap before going to work. Crane would drop her off at Slims.

"Could you possibly pick me up after the party?"

"No problem, but call to remind me. Later," I said.

CHAPTER 8

I was refreshed after my nap. I wanted to dress up a little tonight. Florida is normally so casual. I pulled out a Cold Water Creek long skirt with tropical flowers and palm leaves printed on it. The colors were earth tones. I then picked a light peach peasant blouse that matched the color of the Hibiscus flowers on the skirt. Three-inch wedge scandals in rope and leather were added. I used costume jewelry to accent. I chose a wood necklace from the Islands and long earrings to match. I added some peach lipstick, and my hair was brushed out and fell softly around my shoulders. I was ready.

I filled out a gift card from Baby N U with both Gina and my name in the from column. As I got into the Mustang, I added the card to the gift and headed over to the police station, watching my speed limit.

There was a large conference room off of the main lobby of the police station that was being used to hold the party. This allowed shifts coming on and going off to attend, along with those that had the day off. Whoever was responsible for the decoration had gone all out. Balloons, signs, and crepe paper were hung all over. In one corner was the traditional decorated umbrella. Captain Colson and his wife were well liked. Mr. and Mrs. Colson were enjoying all the fuss that was made over them. If you know cops, food is a big part of any party. Food and drinks were plentiful. Of course, for those working there was plenty of hot coffee. The room was packed already. I entered pushing the bassinette.

Gina approached me as soon as I passed the doorway. She wanted to ogle our present. She clapped her hands in delight. "How cute! You even added a miniature Miss Piggy. Let's get something to drink. You look so elegant, Inga."

I told Gina I liked her dress and killer shoes. "They must be four inch."

Gina can wear a very high heal since she, like her mom, is petite. She has olive coloring, black hair, and piercing brown eyes. Her mouth is naturally a delicate pink. She wears no makeup. That is because it is not necessary. She looks better than Elizabeth Taylor, and we all know what a knockout she is. Gina is also very family-orientated and particular about whom she dates. She is independent, keeping herself busy and being a complete, happy person. She drives a Mini Cooper that is white with black stripes. It does look like a mini patrol car.

The twins, Jay and Steve Burner, for her birthday last year had added long eyelashes to her headlights. When she walked out and saw this spectacle, she went after the twins like a tigress. They impishly removed them. Then she realized that she missed them and insisted they put them back on. Some of the glue had weakened, and now it gave the impression that one eyelash was winking. I heard a rumor that they bought a flashing red light they intended to install for Christmas on the top of her car. They are such devils.

I think you are now seeing the complete picture of our friends, family, and neighbors. We help each other, love each other, and enjoy the company of each other. We are very rich to have this special bond.

I felt a presence. I felt compelled to look up and across the room. My eyes met Tom's. I gulped. The intensity of his stare froze me in place. I could not stop staring. I could not breathe, but that was because I had stopped breathing. My heart was filled to the brim with the purest of joy in just seeing him. I felt that I was standing in a vacuum. There was nothing and no one else in the room. Just Tom and I.

I wished he would do something other than just stare, because I was rooted to where I stood. I definitely could not do anything else. Then I saw a faint smile start to appear on his lips. My body received an electric jolt. I wasn't sure if I was shaking from the jolt or if I was on a weight-reducing machine programmed on high.

My mind registered that the smile was not directed at me but someone approaching him. I can't believe that Betty Perfect is standing in front of him. I now hated her even more than before. She was still up to her old tricks, and here only yesterday I was feeling sorry for her. I reprimanded myself for not having ladylike thoughts and behavior. Then the opening between Tom and I closed, and the spell was broken.

"Inga, what is the matter with you? You look like you saw a ghost," Gina said, shaking me.

"What is Betty Perfect doing here?" I asked Gina.

"She used to be the meter maid, and when they discontinued the meter parking they gave her an administration job. She has been here a long time," Gina commented.

"Did you say she was a meter maid?" I was feeling a little superior.

"Actually," Gina began, "that was a good job. You got to be outside and only worked day hours. No weekends or holidays. And this was supplemental income to her. She was married to an attorney. Then the husband started to fool around with his secretary, and you know the old story. She is recently divorced and having a difficult time."

Now I am feeling the guilt thing again. How could I be such a rotten person? "Thanks for sharing with me," I said.

Just then speakers and radios came to life, stating there was a robbery taking place at Slims.

"Babes is working there tonight. We need to get there on the double." I grabbed Gina's arm. Panicked.

The room was clearing quickly. Gina agreed. We headed for my car. After all, the police and I drove all over town together.

While I waited for Gina to get her purse, I felt a touch on my shoulder. I turned to see Tom standing there with a serious look on his face. I could only stare at his face.

He opened his mouth and sternly said, "Why didn't you tell me about the baby?"

Thankfully my mind started to work, and I felt my mouth loosen up. "Why didn't you attend the final divorce hearing?" I guessed he didn't know I was not there either.

"I just couldn't stand to see it end."

"Tom, I didn't know about the baby until after the divorce. I was only able to carry it for a few months. Then it was gone also." Tears started to stream down my face. My head was down. I noticed Tom's feet start to move toward me. I hurt so badly. A few moments ago my heart was filled with joy, overflowing just with the sight of him, and now I felt my heart was being ripped right out of my body. Without experiencing love, you never know the high and lows of life.

Just then Gina approached. She rushed over when she saw me crying uncontrollably. Tom said he needed to leave and was gone.

"Come on. Let's check on Babes." Gina had put her arms around me.

She drove my car, and this time I didn't care what speed we were going.

CHAPTER 9

As we drove toward Slims, and once I calmed down, I dialed my sister to tell her about the robbery. Gina asked me to mention to her to call her mom and explain what happened also. This seemed to be a good idea so that no one would be worrying about us. I would tell Borgs about Tom later.

We could hear the sirens and saw the flashing lights as we got closer. Thank God they were not after me. It seemed to be quite a distance away we had parked. We walked quickly to get to the restaurant. I didn't think we would be able to get near Babes with all the police present. Slims was well known in the area, and everyone enjoyed their food.

They also were famous for having lizards with the curly tails. This may sound silly, but it is a must-see sight. Babes spotted us, and before anyone could stop her, she had reached us and had her arms tightly around us. They graciously allowed us to stay with her. I'm sure they realized it was calming her down. So we were present when Babes got to tell her side of the story.

She was working the left section of the restaurant, which was a smaller area, and almost all the customers were gone. She was busy cleaning up and actually was under a table picking up some trash that was not swept up.

That is when she heard. "Stick them up. This is a robbery," a male voice said.

She thought, *Is this for real?* Babes knew anyone entering the restaurant would never have seen her, and maybe she was the only chance of capturing this bad guy. She figured the man was facing the cash register and would have his back to her. She poked her head up and confirmed this was true.

Nervous, she started blowing a huge bubble and noticed the rolled napkin silverware packet sitting on top of the table. Babes grabbed it and quietly got to her feet and approached the robber from the rear.

She got directly behind the robber and jammed the silverware packet into his back and said, "Drop it."

Startled, he raised his arms. Still holding the gun, he turned his head into Babe's giant bubble. The glasses he was wearing adhered to the gum and lifted off his face. He now could not see anything, and that is when the shot rang out, flying the robber's gun into the air. Babes passed out.

The second hero was Officer Mendez, who was just coming out of the bathroom, and again was out of the peripheral vision of the robber. He drew his gun, and once the robber's gun was high enough not to hurt anyone, he aimed and shot the gun while it was in motion. It turned out that Officer Mendez was a crack shot.

Chief Walters was very pleased that no one was hurt, and he had something to commend Officer Mendez for. They had the robber in cuffs and were interrogating him in the back of the restaurant.

Officer Mendez spotted Babes and approached her. "May I thank you for your bravery? My name is Rolando Mendez, and yours is?"

"Bobblehead."

"You are Bobblehead?" he answered sounding shocked.

Babes looked at him and sweetly nodded her head.

"I apologize. May I please buy you a cup of coffee?" he said very sincerely.

Looking at Officer Mendez's sexy Cuban good looks, Babes graciously agreed to have coffee with him, not one to hold grudges when it comes to a handsome guy.

It was then that the restaurant door opened, and we could hear motorcycles arriving. In walks Slim with a big smile on his face. We could see he was relieved no one was hurt and also no money was missing. Next to appear were the twins, Mama Rosa, and Borgs. Behind them was the crew from the Pie.

The Pie crew had heard about the robbery from Biscayne Park Police, who had stopped by at the Pie for pizza. Biscayne Park was just north of Miami Shores. Biscayne Park was known for their posted road signs: "Don't even think of speeding." I needed to adapt that motto or stop thinking.

Our employees were concerned for the staff of Slims and had come to help. Mama Rosa had awakened the twins. They gallantly offered her a ride on their Harley. Then Borgs called Mama Rosa and asked for them to pick her up too. I told you we were a close group.

Crane was still at basketball practice and was shooting also, only the calmer basketball version. We all grabbed booths next to each other and ordered breakfast, but not before all new arrivals gave Babes a hug and made sure she was all right.

Slim joined the police and soon found out that the robber only had a toy gun and was also homeless. The police called him Homey. He was down on his luck and needed food. Slim immediately had the cook make a big breakfast for Homey and then announced everyone else could order breakfast on the house.

We immediately ordered more, not to hurt his feelings.

Chief Walters stopped by Babe's booth and thanked her personally for her courage and said how happy he was that she was not harmed. He then reminded Officer Mendez that he was still on duty and at his leisure to please return to the station and complete his report. I was his next stop.

Leaning in close to my ear, he whispered, "You really shook my brother up tonight." He then kissed me on the cheek.

I turned pink. In parting he announced that Slim would not press charges and had also hired Homey to help in the kitchen. We all cheered for Homey's good fortune. As we waited for breakfast we decided to have a meeting about the Pointe's potluck dinner we planned for Sunday night.

Mama Rosa again insisted on making trays of lasagna for us. Borgs said she would provide pies for dessert. The twins said they would handle all the drinks and ice. Babes offered to bring Italian bread and cheese for pre-dinner snacks. I followed up by offering all the paper goods and salad.

I asked the twins if they were planning entertainment. They grinned ear to ear and said we were having a Chicken Dance contest. They had played their guitars over in Goodland last weekend, which is on the west coast of Florida and had been part of their Chicken Dance contest. They often played gigs for local restaurants and were well known.

Mama Rosa clapped her hands and said she would participate and offered Gina and me as co-contestants. The twins only grinned more. I had an uneasy feeling about this contest, but with all plans made, I reminded everyone of the Halloween costume contest on Saturday.

Jay offered the use of their Volkswagen van, affectionately called the love bug. This seemed a good idea, since we were gaining in size with all the animals. By this time we had consumed all the food, and it was time to go. There was no bill to pay, so we left a hefty tip.

Officer Mendez offered to drive Babes home. Hmmmm. Jay and Steve hopped on their Harleys.

The Pie crew got in their delivery car, but not before Cabby had pulled me aside and quietly said, "We need to talk about that Fortune Cookie Restaurant."

"I will call you in the morning," I replied.

Borgs, Gina, Mama Rosa, and I got into my chariot. As soon as I got behind the steering wheel I saw a single peach-colored rose on the dash of my car. My heart was bounding with happiness. Tom remembered my favorite color of rose. It was always his way of saying hi.

Everyone saw me pick up the rose and inhale the fragrance. They knew who had left it but decided not to kid me about it. I was looking too happy. I dropped off Borgs and then Mama Rosa. Gina had asked me to take her to the police station to get her car, Winkie! She would need it in the morning.

After I dropped off Gina I headed back by the Fortune Cookie. I wanted to check out the back entrance to the restaurant and see if surveillance was again taking place. Yep, there was the shadow. An apartment complex was alongside the Fortune Cookie separated by a road running behind the restaurant, a fence, and then a road swinging next to and alongside the apartment building.

I thought, *This is where the action is taking place.* This is where I intended to be tomorrow night. I preceded home, not really concerned with the speed limit since most of the police force was tied up with the recent robbery.

I went to sleep smelling the fragrance of a rose placed next to my bed.

CHAPTER 10

I awoke to the ringing of my phone. I was thinking, *This is an ungodly time to call someone*, until I glanced at the clock as I was reaching for the phone. It read 9:00 a.m. I tried to make my voice sound awake and cordial as I answered the phone with, "Good morning."

"Still asleep? Vacation must be agreeing with you."

I recognized Jack Turner's voice. He was the director of aviation for the Miami International Airport. I was a bit surprised over his call.

"All right, you caught me sleeping in. I am glad you called so I don't waste this vacation day sleeping."

"I hate to disturb your much-earned time off, but I need a favor. I have already gotten approval from your people, and if you agree they will extend your vacation time. Here is the deal: the Boston Patriot football team has chartered a United Airlines jet to fly them down from Boston early Thursday evening." Jack was rattling on.

"If you could deadhead up to Boston prior to their take off and then accompany the flight down, I would not expect you to work the flight. Just do some of your great public relations work during the flight. Maybe a list of fun things to do. Upon arrival I want you to join me and the Patriots' coach and quarterback along with the Dolphins coach and quarterback for a televised friendly rival competition. I thought after we finished the interview you and I could take in dinner in the Grove. I know this is a lot to decipher when you just woke up. Want to call me back?'

"No, Jack, I am following. I can do this for you, but I will not commit to dinner. Is that okay?"

I knew Jack must have been up most of the night trying to figure an angle for a date. It was getting difficult to side step him without feelings getting in the way. It is not that he isn't good looking; it is just that something may be wrong after three divorces, and he was only forty years old.

We agreed to touch bases later to confirm details. I called UAL dispatch and asked for a deadhead pass to Boston tomorrow and available times.

I then headed for the coffee maker and dialed Cabby. He answered right away. He was as worked up over the Fortune Cookie, as I was.

"There is something wrong with that operation, and I am afraid it is drugs. I just don't know what to do about it. I am concerned about our school kids." His worried voice said.

I agreed with Cabby. I suggested that we work out a plan for tonight. Since he was off we could observe the action taking place at the rear of the store.

"Let's wait until dark. Can you get to a spy store?" I asked. "We need a night camera and night-vision glasses. We should be dressed in black."

"No problem. I will pick you up in the Pie car," Cabby said.

I reminded him, "Not a word to my sister."

"I see no evil. I hear no evil. I speak no evil."

"Good, that certainly covers everything. Later."

I then gave Borgs a call to see if she wanted to go to the pumpkin patch at the Miami Shores Presbyterian Church. "We love this event, and we could buy for the Pie, your house, and the Pointe," I told Borgs.

She agreed for that afternoon when they opened.

I quickly showered and put on some jeans and a loose T-shirt with pumpkins on the front. After a quick breakfast I headed over to the library to pick up a good book to read on my vacation and the flight to Boston.

Upon entering the library, I waved to the twins and asked where I would find the mystery section.

"That is a mystery. You need to follow the clues," they said as they pointed toward the back area.

I keep an alphabetized-by-author loose-leaf on all the books I have read. I am a profuse reader and have at times picked up a book I have already read. It really isn't a big deal, since I normally don't remember what happened and need to read it again anyway. The record keeping just cuts down on the occurrences.

I was looking for my favorite authors when I heard this sniffling. It started to get louder as I went in search of the sound. Huddled in a corner with shoulders hunched and her back to me was, of all people, Betty Perfect. I didn't know what was best—to approach or go away. I decided to try and help. After all, everyone needs someone.

I came forward and spoke softly so as not to frighten her. "Betty, it is Inga. I was in the next aisle and happened to hear you. Can I help?"

Much to my surprise Betty was glad to see me. "Inga, I need to talk with someone who is a friend and can help me," she said.

Now I knew she was dimensional. This was worse than I thought. "Betty, we have known each other a long time. How can I help? I am a good listener."

Betty began with her marriage going on the rocks. The divorce and then her low esteem of her self-value. She wanted a temporary prop. She felt herself sliding. Betty checked some of the files on record at the police station and got names of suppliers. At first the intake was controlled but quickly became demanding to her system. Then she heard of the Fortune Cookie as the best place to get what she needed. My ears perked up with this news.

"How does it work?" I said. All ears but not bunny ones.

"New customers stop by the restaurant and pick up a fortune cookie. They place their credit card information on a slip of paper and what they want, along with their phone number, and place it in the cookie. They give this to the cashier. Going forward, all they need is to call in an order, and it is delivered," Betty told me.

"I am so embarrassed. I can't lose my job. I can't afford the drugs, and I can't control my intake. I am a mess. I need help. Please, Inga, don't tell anyone."

"We can fix this. I believe that the force has a medical clause in their policy to give assistance to employees with substance abuse," I said while giving her a hug.

I wasn't sure of this, but most major medical policies have this provision.

"This way you won't lose your job, and they will pay for your treatment. You need to be sincere in your desire to help yourself and stick to the program. Before you go back to work let's call your health care company and explain the problem. We can use my car so no one will overhear you. Tell them you need to see a doctor right away and be placed in a program. This should give you the support you need to overcome this. If you need time off they will contact your supervisor, and it will be dealt with in strictest confidence. Betty, I will not discuss this with anyone who will hurt you."

We hugged again. Then Betty announced she needed to freshen up before returning to work.

"Naturally, we must at all times look our best," I said. Somehow it didn't sound very nice even to my ears.

I dropped Betty off at the station. She seemed so relieved after the call. She now had direction and hope, a good combination.

I headed back home—watching the speed limit. I was a little exhausted from this emotional drain but happy and hungry.

CHAPTER 11

After lunch I started for the door and heard, "Ripper."

"All right, Ripper, you can come."

He did a quick bathroom break and hopped on my shoulder. I picked Borgs up, and guess who was with her? Yes, the attitude goose Greta. Once settled in, I told her about Tom being at the baby shower and what was said. She said she was glad I told her. She noticed the rose last night on the dash but didn't dare say anything. I then in confidence told her about Betty Perfect.

"I am not surprised. She had that down look about her. I am so proud of you, Inga, for helping her. By the way, her last name is Brager," Borgs said.

"Gee, I never knew that. Go figure."

We parked in the back of the church. Then headed for the pumpkins, which were displayed on the front lawn. What a sight. I could hardly contain my excitement. We started to gather the most perfectly shaped pumpkins. This took a lot of looking. The stems had to be just perfect too.

Greta strutted around. The parents took pictures of her, and she posed with their children. Greta was a sweet goose. The helpers had offered us a wagon since our pile was getting rather large. We ended up pretty much covering the entire patch and were getting close to the discard pile that they had thrown the rotting pumpkins on.

Someone said, "Hi," and as I looked up I saw a flying pumpkin coming straight at me.

I took it in the stomach, and the force pushed me back into an elderly woman behind me who lost her balance and fell into the rotten pile. I heard the laughing but was more concerned with the woman who was yelling, "Get off me, you clumsy jerk!"

More laughter. I was trying to help the elderly women up and turned to offer my hand, but was then hit in the rear with another pumpkin. Yes, I lost my balance again and landed back on top of Big Mouth.

Big Mouth was also large in size and was well padded, which was in our favor. I rolled off of her and looked up into a very familiar face. What first came to my mind was the similarity of voice and look to the Menace kids.

"Do you have a brother and sister named Dennis and Denise?" I said.

"Oh, you have met my sister and brother. My name is Danny." He grinned.

I thought, *Whoever named these kids was not joking.* "Yes, and I met your grandmother."

By this time Big Mouth was on her hands and knees struggling to get up. She was still screaming at me for being clumsy. I let her struggle. I was having enough trouble myself. Everyone naturally heard Big Mouth and was rushing our way, including Greta and Borgs.

I thought I noticed Bear off to the right on the sidewalk without Kelly. That is when Danny pulled out the slingshot from one pocket and what looked like a water pistol from the other pocket. He picked up some rotten pumpkin pieces and aimed them at the oncoming crowd and fired.

Everyone screamed, Big Mouth included. She was shot with the water pistol. Only the water was died orange. I guess the color was appropriate for the season. She took this in the chest.

I was now on my feet and was trying to tackle Danny. I instead got a rotten missile splattered on my face. I gathered Big Mouth did also; only she inhaled hers. It does not pay to be a Big Mouth. It did stop her from screaming at me.

Ripper let go of a curdling loud scream. Greta looked at Danny, and that was all it took. She stretched her neck forward and charged. Danny, not being familiar with geese, didn't know how to handle the charge. So he quickly turned and retreated. His speed of departure was increased when Ripper also went after him and started to peck on his head. Bear joined in on the chase, happy to be part of the fun. Bear was quickly closing in on Danny.

It was a beautiful sight to see him running at top speed and saying, "I'm sorry! I didn't mean it!" Really!

All it took was a mad goose, Pony Dog, and a baby parrot. Crime does not pay.

We called to Greta, Bear, and Ripper to stop. Ripper jumped on Greta's head and rode the way back. Bear trotted along next to Greta. They all got pats and "atta girl" and "atta boy" congratulations.

"How do you know that Pony Dog?" Borgs looked at me and said.

I could hear the sirens in the distance. I took advantage of the distraction and suggested to Borgs that it was time for us to pay up and go home.

"I agree we should pay up, but you need to get under a hose before you can get in a car," Borgs said.

I was then dragged to the closest hose that Borgs could find and literally hosed down. I looked for Big Mouth. She needed this as well. We proceeded to pay and start to leave when Chief Walters rounded the corner. Again he had a big grin on his face.

His opening remark was, "Is the church holding a wet T-shirt contest?"

I tried to dodge him, but I heard a camera snap before I made it. His last few words were, "Nice pumpkins." He was not looking at our wagon. Fresh!

Borgs wrapped me in a towel and decided to drive. We dropped the Pie's supply of pumpkins off first and then went to Borg's house.

After unloading, Borgs gave me a hug and said, "You need to get home. Take a shower and stay home tonight. Curl up with your mystery book."

I agreed wholeheartedly. Now Borgs would not be wondering what I was up to. I needed to get home and get help with the remaining pumpkins and look for some black clothing.

CHAPTER 12

Rustling through my closest, I came up with a cat costume from a past Halloween. I thought this would be perfect. I hoped it still fit. I tried it on and checked it out in the mirror. It would do. Problem solved. I then hopped in the shower and afterward took a nap.

When I awoke it was getting dark. I called Cabby and asked if he was able to get everything we needed. His answer was yes and that he was getting dressed. He would be over shortly. I rushed to get into my cat outfit.

The mask covered my eyes and had pointed ears. My hands were covered with only the fingers exposed. This was good, because I would need them for handling objects. I added black sneakers to complete the outfit.

It was now pitch dark, but as I went to leave I heard, "Ripper."

"Ripper, if you come you will have to be very quiet."

He did the quick bathroom break and was on my shoulder in a flash.

When I got downstairs Cabby was waiting. I got in the Pie car and glanced over at Cabby. He was decked out in a camouflage uniform with a blackened face. He said since he wore this in the army to hide from the enemy it would be perfect for tonight. He was also wearing a helmet, possibly to protect him from falling coconuts. I asked how the old uniform fit.

"A little tight," he answered.

Oh dear.

"Take a look at our supplies." Cabby proudly pointed to.

As I looked through there was a camera and two night-vision glasses, water, and K rations. K rations?

"Cabby where did you get K rations?"

"It was with my uniform."

"Did you check the expiration date?"

"I didn't see one. So I guess they don't expire."

Oh dear!

"Cabby, we need to take the road that runs alongside the apartment building behind the Fortune Cookie. There is a tree right on the border of the two properties. Park the car under the tree, and we can use the roof of the truck to get up higher into the tree."

"Let's put on our glasses, and I will hang the camera around my neck," Cabby said as he parked the truck.

"Wow, these glasses are really great," I mentioned.

I saw a little smile on Cabby's face. He had done well.

"Be very quiet. Help me up unto the roof of the car. Thank you. Cabby, give me your hand, and I will help you up."

I then heard *rrrip*. Oh dear. "Cabby, are you okay?"

"I am okay, but there is a problem with this outfit. The back seam gave way. On the other hand, I can breathe now, and my stomach is calming down."

I'm glad he was calming down. I was a nervous wreck. "I hear a truck pulling around. You have the camera. Can you push aside the hedge and get a picture of the license plate?'

"Yeah, but don't look at my back end."

"I can't see it." Maybe I can. "Are you wearing white underwear?"

"You are peeking.'

"No, it's just the glasses you got are fantastic."

The linen truck pulled to a stop, and two oriental men got out. They looked around and then rapped on the door, saying, "Delivery."

The door swung open, and out came a young man pushing a cart. One of the truck guys said, "Hurry up. We don't want to be out here long with this merchandise."

"How much is this delivery worth?" the cart pusher asked.

His answer was to mind his own business.

Cabby moved into a better position, pushing farther into the hedge and making a slight rustle.

The truckers both stopped in their tracks and, looking at each other, said, "What was that?"

I froze. It actually was the same position I had been in all the time. I guess fear does that. Now Ripper let out a soft parrot sound and flipped his wings a bit.

The taller driver smiled and said, "Just a parrot trying to get close to his mate. After all, this is Florida. Not a bad idea. Finish up, and we'll go look for some mates of our own."

The cart pusher signed and headed inside with a full cart of linens. He closed the back door. The truck drivers were off in a flash.

"Did you get pictures?" I asked and let out my breath.

"It couldn't have been better timing. I got everything we needed. It is time for us to caboose. Uh oh. My pants are caught on the hedge, and when I turned the front ripped." Cabby sounded worried.

"No problem with a little rip," I said.

"That is the problem. It was a big rip, and I don't have my uniform pants anymore."

Oh dear. "Well, just help me down, and we can leave."

I went to pet Ripper on the head for his quick response when I felt a tug. It appeared my long cat tail had attached to the tree. It was then that headlights appeared in the driveway of the apartment we were parked at. Two women wearing hats were in the front seat looking like they had just came from a prayer meeting. They rolled down their windows and asked us to move.

Cabby waved trying to defuse the situation with friendliness and take their attention away from his abbreviated attire. I heard the driver say, "Lord, preserve us."

It appeared that this had happened often by the looks of them.

"That man is not wearing any pants. Is that a young girl up in the tree? How disgusting. Maybe we should get out and help her?" the driver commented to the passenger.

"No, we need to stay in the car. I am dialing the police." the passenger replied.

They started to lay on the horn. Feisty group.

"Quick, get down here," Cabby whispered.

"I am trying to. My tail is caught on a branch," I said a bit exasperated.

Just then the tail came loose. I lost my balance and landed across the chef with the pies on top of the truck. My rear end was stuck up high over the two pies with my cat tail swaying like an antenna. My hands were out in front holding onto the chef's shoes, and my legs and feet covered his rear end.

The ladies were bug-eyed. The passenger with the cell phone yelled into it that a huge black panther had just fallen from the tree and was ready to attack them. There was a pause. Then, "Of course we have not been drinking."

Cabby jumped in the truck and took off. He accelerated so fast that I was plastered against the chef and hanging on for dear life. The corners were the worst. I prayed that the chef stayed on top of the truck. Then I heard the sirens in the distance. Cabby quickly pulled behind a close building. The police passed by at a higher speed then we were traveling. After they passed Cabby got me down and back into the car. We pulled out and drove back to the Pointe. The speed limit was not an issue.

Cabby did not linger in his abbreviated outfit. He was quite embarrassed. I, on the other hand, was not feeling that well after our close scrape with the law.

I told Cabby to keep the pictures. We would review them later.

We both looked at each other and in unison said, "Don't tell Borgs."

There was a floral box at the bottom of the stairs with my name on it when I entered the Pointe. I grabbed it and staggered up the stairs. As I walked in my apartment, my phone was ringing. I forced myself toward the ringing monster. It could be Borgs checking up on me. What a pleasant surprise to hear Tom's voice.

"Inga, I just saw a strange sight outside of your building. A black cat on two paws just went staggering into the building. Also there was a BOLO being broadcast about a large black vicious panther on the prowl. You wouldn't know anything about this by chance?"

I knew he knew that I knew everything about this. Instead I countered with, "Are you watching my building?"

"Of course not. I just dropped off something for you and was pulling away when I saw this strange sight. I called to see if you were safe in your apartment and free for diner tomorrow evening." Now he knew that I knew that he knew.

Please, heart, stop pounding so I can think. My legs were already giving out. I needed something to function on my body. "I am traveling to Boston and back tomorrow. I should be back in the Shores between 7:00 and 8:00 p.m. would that be too late?"

"That is perfect. I will book us for the Shores Country Club for 8:00 p.m. They have entertainment on Thursday evenings. Would you like me to pick you up?"

"It will be less pressure for me just to meet you there in case I am running late."

He ended the conversation with, "Until tomorrow night, blondie."

I didn't need my legs to function anymore. I just floated into the bathroom to take my shower. I placed my second peach-colored rose from the floral box in the vase next to my bed and fell into sweet dreams.

CHAPTER 13

My first phone call the next morning was from Cabby, who said excitedly, "The pictures are perfect. We have the van with the license plate and both guys from the van. We also have a shot of the cart with the linens and the waiter signing for them. What we need now is to get inside and see what is in those linens. We know, but we need proof."

"Oh, Cabby, what a productive night. I will look into our next step and let you know. You are working tonight. What about your expenses?"

"If this works out I will be happy to pay. It will be worth every cent just to put these bad guys away," Cabby remarked with pride in his voice.

"I can't agree with you more, but let me at least pay half so I am part of this also."

"Okay, Skipper. Later."

I grabbed a cup of coffee and started making my plans. First, a pedicure at Profiles with May. If you needed to know any gossip, this was the place to go in the Shores.

Next, a hair appointment with Pat at Wild Hair. He is the best! I intended to wear my uniform to Boston and back, so that simplified things. Now for the evening attire. This had to be perfect. I selected a sundress, sexy and elegant. The top was aqua. The color brought out my eyes. Spaghetti straps with an off-white lace skirt. Short but not too short. The only jewelry was very long aqua-colored earrings and lots of silver and aqua bracelets to match. Taupe leather wedge shoes and a small taupe purse.

Now that all the planning was done, I needed to get on the move. I headed off to my appointments. Back home, I took a quick shower and put my stewardess uniform on and headed out to MIA.

I stopped by UAL dispatch to touch bases and say hi to everyone. I took out my cell and called Jack to confirm the details. I was running very close in time and quickly went to embark on my plane.

The flight up was quiet. I got to read some of my mystery book and make a list of fun things to do in Miami. Once in Boston the show was on. I waved hi to the cockpit crew, and I met with the stewardesses who would be working the flight. Their names were Judi and Sue. I chatted a bit with them to make them more relaxed.

"What are you planning to do on your layover?"

"We are hoping to have a date with one of the Patriots," they said as they both giggled.

The boarding agent let us know that he would be bringing on board the team. In another half hour we were in the air. I was very impressed with the Patriots. They settled down and got busy with what they had planned to do on their flight to Miami. Some were enjoying kidding with each other, and others wanted information from me on places to go while in Miami, which was limited in time.

Of course, South Beach came up. True to form, they hit on Judi and Sue, who both made dates. I turned down my offer. The coach was huddled with the other coaches reviewing strategy and last-minute details. Before I knew it we were putting our seatbelts on and did a perfect three-point landing in Miami.

Jack Turner met the plane, and I introduced him to the Patriot coach Bill Belichick and quarterback Tom Brady. I saw the TV cameras off to the side. Already in place were the Dolphin's coach Joe Philibin and quarterback Ryan Tannehill. Everyone was in a hurry except Jack.

I was placed in the center next to Jack. I was told that would prevent any threats from getting out of hand, and we all laughed. In comparison to everyone in this group, I felt like a midget; if the camera was zeroed in on their faces I would most likely not be in the picture.

The coaches shook hands. Jack asked them if they had any interesting plays worked out that they could disclose. The Patriot coach said he had a dance instructor teaching his linemen how to discreetly stick out their feet to trip the

Dolphins up. The Dolphins coach said that wouldn't help, because he was teaching his linemen the slide step. Smiles all around.

The Dolphins quarterback Tannehill looked at the Patriots quarterback Brady and asked how he planned to handle his defeat on Saturday night.

"Oh, that will be easy, since it will be overshadowed with our celebration. We in Boston do not consider defeat an option. Check our record. Let me personally extend an invitation to you and your team to our celebration party."

More smiles. Forced smiles from the quarterbacks. Now I knew why I was in the middle. Jack turned to me and asked if I favored any particular team. Just like Jack to throw me a curve ball in front of how many million people. I was still in my uniform and representing United Airlines, so I figured I better say something quickly.

"Well, since I am smaller than anyone else here, I think it would be in my best interest not to side with either team."

Just then both quarterbacks stepped forward, and each grabbed me under my arms and lifted me to their level. All three of us were now eyeball to eyeball.

"That was very uplifting," I said. "I wish both teams good luck, since every winning team has always needed a little luck also."

Both quarterbacks leaned toward me and gave me a kiss on the cheek. Flashes from cameras went crazy. More smiles from everyone this time. The conference was over.

Jack was tied up shaking hands, and I used that opportunity to abandon ship.

It was approaching 7:00 p.m., and I still had to get home, change, and be at the club by 8:00 p.m. I made it to the Pointe by 7:30 p.m. I took a quick shower and got dressed. I was beginning to feel like I was on a swim team with all this water. The last touch was a squirt of Brighton perfume called Live. An extra squirt for good luck. I hesitated considering one more squirt but then decided I may be pushing it. Good thing there was valet parking at the club.

When I walked in the door it was exactly 8:00 p.m. I headed for the lounge.

CHAPTER 14

I stopped at the entrance of the lounge and looked around for Tom. I saw him getting up from a table next to a window across the room. He had spotted me also. The club's staff is very friendly and immediately acknowledged me, saying they had just seen me on channel 7. They thought the interview was great. I was stopped by a few neighbors also as I headed toward Tom, who remarked on the great interview. My entrance could not have been grander.

When I reached Tom I thought how impressive he looked. He was six foot five inches tall and buff. He was wearing a sports jacket in blue with an open button-down collared shirt in light blue, matching his eyes. He wore a gold cross around his neck and had tan pants and brown loafers with no socks.

The Shores Country Club is beautiful at night. They have lights accented in the landscape that create a warm and romantic mood. My mood was already romantic, but this added to it. Tom did also. I was nervous. Would I live through this? I had dreamed of this moment for so long. It meant everything to me. It had to work.

"I selected a table for four since I can sit next to you rather than across from you." Tom said as he was pulling out my chair.

How sweet. I saw a peach single rose in a vase on our table.

Tom sat down and quickly put his arm behind my chair, leaned in, and kissed me on the cheek. "I took the liberty of ordering a bottle of wine, which I hope you will enjoy."

"Delicious," I said after taking a sip and smiled.

The three-piece band started to play soft music. The waiter appeared with menus, and we started to look them over.

"Now that I am looking at a menu, I realize I am starved," I said.

Tom smiled and said he enjoyed my appetite. "Let's order. Then we can relax."

I ordered chicken marsala, and Tom ordered rib-eye steak, medium. We both asked for small Caesar salads.

Tom then surprised me by producing a square white box from his jacket. He handed this to me as he opened the lid. I was totally surprised and pleased when I looked inside. It was a beautiful silver chain, and hanging in the middle was a fortune cookie, also in silver. I was speechless.

He looked in my eyes and said, "I consider myself fortunate to be here with you, and I wanted you to know how much this means to me. May I help you put it on?"

My heart was filled with happiness. I nodded my agreement for his help.

"Would you humor me and not take it off? I would like to imagine you wearing this." Tom surprised me with this comment.

"If this makes you happy, I will keep it on, but I adore it, so it will not be difficult," I said as I placed my hand on the fortune cookie.

Our salads arrived, and we both dug in. The rest of the diner was served efficiently and was delicious.

When the dishes were cleared Tom took my hand. "I didn't know you would be on TV today. You downplayed your trip to Boston. That was a good shot at the end with both quarterbacks kissing you on either cheek. I was a little jealous."

"Tom, I have done a lot of thinking over these last two years. We have been apart, and I think I have come to good decisions about commitments. It can't be all parties without more meaning than that. I guess I have grown up. I feel if two people want to commit to each other and spend their lives together and this commitment is made before God, family, and friends, than it should also have meaning— whether that be raising children in a good family environment or committing to a common goal that benefits others, or even having individual goals that are respected by both.

"Then there is a meaning to the relationship. It creates higher challenges and standards to grow into as a couple and also individually. Love should not be selfish. It should be shared with others to help them or to bring them happiness they may not have. Love cannot be dormant. It must grow to flourish and be everything that dreams are made of. It makes the day exciting to get up to and a future to strive for. A love to be jealous of. It can only be these things when it is valued and preserved as precious. Only then does the union make sense, because love is a beautiful gift." I stopped.

"I am sorry I got carried away. I didn't mean to say this. It just came out, but I meant every word."

Tom looked in my eyes and said, "I am so proud of you for saying what was in your heart and for placing such a high value to the love of two people. These are words I hoped you would feel and believe. I have done a lot of thinking also. I want value to my life. The person I share that with I want to have those values also. Enough seriousness. I know you want to move slowly, and I will respect that. I look forward to future conversations. I also want you to know again how fortunate I feel to be here with you. Please keep the necklace on."

"Tom, I love it. I will not take it off."

Tom leaned forward and gave me a light kiss on the lips. I wanted more. I was starved for love.

"It is getting late." He handed me my rose. "Let me follow you home to make sure you arrive safely."

Tom's black Porsche Carrera was parked along the curb in front of the country club, but my classic convertible was parked right behind it.

Tom opened my door and said, "Good night, blondie," after a quick kiss.

As we pulled in front of the Pointe, Tom beeped his horn and took off. As I drove around to the garage I thought that this was the right time to bring up such heavy thoughts. It was best to get it out up front. Then everyone can go from there. Do not settle for second best. Tom was too precious.

I parked the car and turned to walk out of the garage when I saw what looked like a scarecrow or a drunk hanging from the lamppost across the street, but as I stared at it longer I realized it was human and it was Homey. He was not moving. That is when I screamed and fainted.

CHAPTER 15

I opened my eyes and saw a vision before me. He was so hot he was smoking. His eyes were an intense dark brown. Lots of black hair. A roman nose and lips with an olive color. I could feel the strength of his arms. His mouth was inches from mine. I could see smoke spiraling around his head. I could not speak or move. I felt the heat. I thought I would call him Smokey.

I could hear Bob's voice. "It was an execution-style killing. Do you think it meant anything that he was placed on the lamppost across the street from the Pointe?"

I thought, *What does that mean?*

"What do you think? Look at the position of his hand. It looks like it is pointing in that direction. Who is that guy holding Inga?" That was Tom's voice.

"Tom, you look like steam is coming out of your ears watching him. Did you get the plant on Inga? Did you call Borgs?" Bob said.

Tom answered yes to both.

I thought, *What does that mean?*

"That guy holding Inga is the Washington Federal Agent you are dealing with. He just arrived. Here is the medic," Bob informed Tom.

I thought, *What does that mean?*

Smokey was replaced by Shores Fire Rescue Team. "How is she?" I heard Borg's voice ask.

"She hit her head pretty hard on the cement. She could have a concussion. We will need to take her to North Shore Hospital. Do you want to ride with us?" the medic responded.

"Yes. Tom, can you get someone to bring my car to the hospital?" Borgs answered.

"Not a problem. I will meet you there."

"I see she is hanging onto a peach rose. That must be a good sign." Borgs smiled.

What seemed like hours later I at last received a visit from the emergency room doctor. I also got to meet Nurse Bulldog. Nurse Bulldog had a flattened face with droopy eyes and mouth. I could not tell about her hair, since she was wearing a nurse's cap. Her arms actually came forward and hung slightly bent like a bulldog.

Everyone was in the room—Gina, Mama Rosa, Babes, Crane, Jay, Steve, Chief Bob, and Tom, along with the Pie crew. I noticed Cabby watching me closely. The twins said when I let out the scream Ripper began his own screaming. They rushed upstairs to my apartment, and as soon as they opened the door, oops forgot to lock it again, Ripper took off in search of me.

I heard a soft, "Ripper." Jack flashed his jacket open a fraction, and I saw Ripper's head poke out.

Nurse Bulldog then started barking orders. "She is heavily sedated and will need to sleep. Everyone needs to say good-bye and leave *now*."

I still could not talk or move. Unobserved Jack slipped Ripper under my pillow, positioned so he would not get crushed. Pretty soon the room was empty except for Borgs, Bob, and Tom. Borgs said she called United Airlines and spoke with my boss. My vacation was extended another month. Tom smiled. Borgs asked Tom if they should stay all night.

Nurse Bulldog answered that was not necessary. She would handle everything. Both Tom and Bob agreed with Nurse Bulldog they should all go home and get some sleep.

Tom leaned over and moved my hospital gown by my neck a bit to make sure I still had on the necklace. He then kissed me flat on the lips. I could feel the salt on my lips as his tears touched my face and ran down my cheeks. I then fell into a deep sleep.

I was awakened to whispering. I saw two Chinese men who looked like the linen van drivers from the Fortune Cookie restaurant. This was odd. They argued for a while. I could not make out what was said. An occasional word like "smother" or was it "strangle reached my ears."

As they reached for my IV, Nurse Bulldog charged in, and at the same time Ripper emerged sounding a scary parrot call and took flight. Nurse Bulldog was stunned by Rippers appearance and stopped in her tracks. Ripper was persistent and started to head for the Chinese driver's eyes.

I never saw two people try to get through a door at the same time and insistent to be first. It was even more difficult since they had their faces covered with their hands to protect their eyes from Ripper. They kept bumping into each other until Nurse Bulldog gave each of them a swift kick in the pants, sending them both through the door at the same time, squeezed sideways together. Ripper returned to perch on the head frame of my bed.

Nurse Bulldog continued after them, screaming, "Not on my watch! Get out!"

Upon returning, Nurse Bulldog looked at Ripper and said, "You are better than a security guard with a gun."

I heard, "Ripper," and I faded out.

I awoke to a flapping of wings. As my vision cleared, I saw it was Tully. He smiled when he saw my eyes open.

"I didn't want to wake you, Inga. This is just too serious for me not to help. I am talking about the Fortune Cookie restaurant. We have to protect our community. So I am helping. Here is the plan. You should be released tomorrow. Friday night after the Fortune Cookie restaurant closes around 2:00 to 3:00 a.m. I will make sure that the back door is unlocked at the Fortune Cookie."

Tully's actual profession was a banker, but when big chain banks were allowed into Florida and started to buy up the industry, private banking dried up. He found a new career in locksmithing. So this was help we could depend on.

"That is when you and Cabby sneak in. Make sure you bring the camera. Look through the linens. That is where they keep the drugs. Take pictures. Then take a sample with you. Saturday night after the animal Halloween contest stop by the Fortune Cookie to pick up a food order you called in earlier. When they go to get it, find a place to hide the drugs."

"We can then make a unanimous phone call to alert the police to check the restaurant. Make sure you get hold of Cabby tomorrow. Good luck. Go back to sleep. I will be watching your safety tonight. Don't mention this to Borgs."

Just then Nurse Bulldog reappeared and saw Tully. She screamed, "A ghost! A ghost!" and ran for the door as Chief Walter entered pushing the door open, smacking Nurse Bulldog in the face. No wonder she looked like a bulldog.

He then saw her and said, "Nurse, you called me about a security problem? Nurse, you look like you just saw a ghost."

She crumbled to the floor.

I fell back to sleep, a faint smile appearing on my lips.

CHAPTER 16

I awoke to a heavenly scent, a big bouquet of peach roses. Tom was holding one hand, and Borgs was holding the other. Both had concerned looks on their faces. I squeezed both their hands, and smiles appeared on their faces. Well, this was progress. I could move my hands. I wonder if I could talk.

"Water please."

The doctor came in just as I had said that. "You seem to be on the mend," he said. "Let's see how you are doing, and maybe we can get you out of here." He completed his checkup and said, "I am going to release you, but only on the condition that you do not do anything for another twenty-four hours. Complete rest. Am I making myself clear?"

I would have agreed to anything. Borgs hustled Tom out of the room. I said I would shower at home and quickly threw some clothes on. Ripper jumped on my shoulder. A wheelchair arrived pushed by another nurse.

"Please tell my nurse good-bye," I asked the new nurse.

"Once she returns from the leave she was placed on, I will," the new nurse replied.

Really? I didn't think the night was that difficult? She gave Ripper a double take.

Tom took over the wheelchair once all the paperwork was complete. We started for the front door. Borgs waited with me while Tom got his car.

Borgs told me that Tom insisted on taking care of me so she would be only a phone call away if I needed her. She looked down at my roses and commented on how beautiful they were. Tom pulled up and loaded me in. Borgs yelled after us that she would send some pizza pies over for lunch.

Once back at the Pointe, I was able to take that promised shower and put on some lounge wear. Tom insisted I hop in bed. Just then lunch arrived. I was starved. I felt a little ashamed that I ate more than Tom, but there was plenty of food. He would not go hungry.

Tom put a movie on, crawled in next to me, and pulled me into his arms. I fell sound asleep.

I slept well into the afternoon. Mama Rosa had brought up spaghetti and meatballs for our dinner while I slept. Tom was busy answering and making phone calls. He put another movie on, one of my favorites, *Top Draw*. I watched this until dinnertime.

Tom brought me a tray so I could eat in bed. Did life get better than this? Borgs sent over some mile-high pies for dessert. Cabby delivered them.

When we had a minute alone, I told Cabby to meet me back here around 3:00 a.m. "Get rid of the pie chef on top of the smart car, and try and wear a complete camouflage outfit. Especially the pants. Don't forget the camera."

"Are you sure you want to do this?" he blushed as he said this.

"It is a piece of cake or pie. Whatever," I said.

"Don't tell Borgs."

"Are you kidding? I'm like Biscayne Park. I won't even think of telling Borgs."

Tom and I were now watching a *Skinny Man* movie, and it was getting near 10:00 p.m. Tom offered to spend the night.

"I would rather be 100 percent fit when you spend the night, but it is tempting," I said sadly turning down the offer.

"I just want you to know I am here for you."

"Tom, that means so much." I then gave him a kiss that spoke better than words.

With a smile on his face, he said, "Goodnight, blondie. I will call in the morning."

I then concentrated on trying to get some sleep since I had to be back up at 2:00 a.m. It rolled around too quickly. I wanted to stay in bed. Duty called. I took a quick shower to wake me up and put on my trusty cat costume.

Ripper was sound asleep, and I tiptoed out. He had a busy night at the hospital. I was downstairs when Cabby pulled up. I went over the plan with Cabby. He thought this was great.

"How did you get a locksmith to do this?" he asked awed.

"Don't ask, and don't tell," my answer was.

I noticed he was wearing a black sweat suit. Hood and all. If I added ears to the top of his hoodie and a tail to the back of his pants, we would look like two big strutting cats out on the town.

We quickly got to the Fortune Cookie. I told him to pull around the back and turn off the lights. We both had our night-vision glasses on and carried flashlights. Cabby had the camera around his neck. I thought I saw a curtain move from the apartment building next door.

We tried the knob, and it turned. We hurried inside. We went straight for the linen area. Cabby was the first to come across some stash, taking pictures as we went.

"Find a small amount that I can carry," I reminded him.

Soon we had enough pictures and some stash to bring with us. We turned off our flashlights and opened the door. Cabby reached the driver's side first and got in. He started the engine. We then heard police sirens very close. I noticed the curtain from the same apartment building swaying. Busybody!

"We have to get out of here fast! Hang on!" Cabby yelled

I never made it to the car seat before Cabby was moving.

I was hanging onto the door, which was swinging back and forth depending which direction Cabby was driving.

My tail was stuck in the door and hooked unto the antenna. I was thinking about a jaguar and how the cat sits so nicely on the hood. Of course the smart car was smaller, and I was bigger, so maybe it was not a good comparison, since at times when he rounded the corner the door would swing all the way open with me hanging onto the top of the door frame, not the hood, by my fingers. Definitely not a jaguar look. I was also wearing an expression of total fear. I didn't think the jaguar had that expression on its face.

It then started to rain. Cabby found our same hiding place as last time and swung in. He helped me down tenderly.

"Are you okay, Inga?" He probably remembered I was his boss.

"Cabby, I am just having a wonderful time swinging in the rain. Thanks for asking."

We waited a few minutes and decided it was safe. Then we congratulated ourselves on how well that went.

"Piece of cake…or pie," we said and high-fived.

"Cabby, drop me off a block away from my apartment, and I'll sneak back in."

As soon as I reached my apartment, the phone was ringing.

"Just checking to see if everything is okay." My luck it was Tom.

"What could possibly be happening at this hour?" I replied.

"Oh, there was another BOLO on a big panther. Only this time there were two."

"They must be mating."

"That could work." Tom chuckled.

Oops, wrong choice of words. What was that supposed to mean?

CHAPTER 17

There was a message on my answering machine when I awoke the next morning. It was from Borgs saying to give her a call. While I sipped a cup of coffee I dialed her number.

"Good morning, Inga. How are you feeling?"

"Much better," I answered. "I feel like I was never ill. It must be all this rest."

Borgs wanted to know if I would go costume shopping for the animals and then do lunch with her. "We could stop by the Pie and update the good deed board. It is good to keep the contest stirred up to get it going. What do you think?"

I heard a knocking on the door and excused myself. When I answered it, Tom was standing with a big box that smelled sooo good. "Breakfast, blondie." He grinned.

I finished my conversation with Borgs and confirmed a time to meet. Tom was busy laying out all the food on the kitchen table, along with a peach rose. What a spread. Scrambled eggs, bacon, grits, biscuits, and fruit.

"The way to a women's heart is through her stomach. At least yours, blondie."

Maybe I did eat too much lunch yesterday after all. I threw all caution to the wind. After all, I was starved. I sat down and dug in until my stomach yelled, "No more! Please!"

I turned to Tom and said, "You are spoiling me."

"Then the plan is working," he answered.

I told him of my plans with Borgs, which he thought sounded good.

"Are you sure you are up to this?" Inga shook her head yes.

Once that was agreed upon, he said he needed to catch up on work after playing hooky yesterday. I thanked him for breakfast and said I would handle the clean-up. We kissed a lingering kiss and almost forgot our plans made just moments before. A kiss is just not a kiss. A kiss is highly influential. Maybe a sigh is just a sigh.

Once showered, I put on some shorts and a halter-top. I drove over to Borgs and picked her up. She said there was a costume shop on Biscayne Boulevard close to the pet store. I mentioned I might need to go to a doll store to get something tiny enough for Ripper. We didn't see anything too exciting in the costume shop.

"How about the pet shop?" Borgs suggested.

"That's a good idea. They would have perfect sizes too."

We lingered quite a while to make sure we didn't forget someone, and we found the best items and fits.

Satisfied, Borgs suggested we stop by the new pizza place on Northeast 2nd Avenue. "I am anxious to check out our competition."

I was still filled up from breakfast, so I could go anywhere. As soon as we were seated in the restaurant, the owner approached us, I thought maybe to tell us to get out, but no, he was very friendly. He said he had been to our restaurant and enjoyed the food.

"Anytime you want to get rid of your cook, just let me know."

We smiled and said he was not going anywhere. The food and service was good. Borgs and I split a meatball sub. I took the bigger half. We left a big tip since they refused to charge us, and we wished them good luck.

We then headed to the Pie. Cook was asked first if he had done a good deed yet.

"My neighbor got sick, and I cooked for her until she was back on her feet," he said.

Borgs wrote that one down on our bulletin good dead board. When Numbers was asked she said she had not done anything important enough to mention. Hon said her friend fell and she was cleaning the house for her. Borgs wrote that one down also.

Cabby just shook his head, saying, "Nothing yet." Then he winked at me.

I dropped Borgs off and said I needed to take a nap if we were going to have a big evening with the animal costume party tonight. When I got home I called the Fortune Cookie and ordered a lot of food for pick up that evening. I figured we could bring it back to our recreation room and everyone would chow down. Especially me.

Around 5:00 p.m. we started to assemble downstairs. Jay and Steve had the love bug pulled up in front. Their cat, Queenie, was dressed in a long purple robe and was wearing a stunning jeweled tiara. She was cut like a lion.

Mama Rosa and Gina had matching poodles, brother and sister. Both were dressed like pumpkins. They were called Mickey and Minnie.

Babes had a tiger cat that she had sprayed pink and had put a big pink bow on her tail. She had a tutu on and was called Pinks.

Crane also had a gray-and-black striped cat that had white paws. He was wearing a top hat. She called him Dude. Ripper had a little skull hat with cross bones and a skull on it. A little toughie.

We all piled into the love bug. The outside was painted with peace signs and flowers. It even had surfboards strapped to the top. It was vintage and restored well.

We headed for Borgs's house. Added to the group was Annie in a witch's costume complete with black cape and hat. She was the perfect witch because of her long nose. No warts though.

Greta had gotten rid of the bunny ears, at least for the evening, and was dressed as Mother Goose. Borgs then handed up Teel, who had a tiny hat with a flower sticking out. Borgs had a turtle crawl in the backyard next to the house that Tully had built. A neighbor had seen this tortoise swimming in the lake and rescued it. These turtles were not swimmers. They contacted Tully and Borgs. Teel, the tortoise, has been in the turtle crawl since. This tortoise had an appetite like me. It had tripled in size. That is scary!

We now headed for the pet shop. As we pulled in we saw other customers with their pets dressed up for the contest. Bear came in with Kelly and her parents. We all stayed together. Bear and Kelly were dressed as the dancing bear team. Kelly had the organ. Bear was himself with a stupid grin on his face every time he looked toward Annie.

Annie tried to look coquettish with a witch's hat on. This was not easy to do, but somehow she succeeded. Borgs was sending evil witch looks my way. Maybe she should have been dressed as the witch? I put a distant look on my face and said nothing in memory of Shultz.

The twins had a twinkle in their eye. I knew trouble was headed are way. They positioned themselves at the end of the aisle with one of them on each side. In walked a rather large woman with a huge St. Bernard dressed as a nurse. It was hard to tell who was larger. The twins invited her to stand in front of the aisle and asked what the Palmetto's name was.

The women smiled and said, "You must be joking. This is not a horse. It is a dog. Her name is Nurse Betty."

Then one of the twins began to engage her in conversation while the other kept feeding Nurse Betty treats. What was in the barrel around her neck? Had she ever rescued anyone? Did she know Lassie?

The woman was getting a little flustered. Then they tapped her on the other shoulder. She turned to see an identical person that she had just been talking to but on the opposite side. They were both dressed alike. When they dress alike it normally means trouble. The woman was starting to get dizzy from constantly turning from one side to the other side to talk with the same person. Nurse Betty was being stuffed with treats and looking restless.

The judging began. It went along quickly. Everyone received a metal on a cloth necklace placed around their neck. I'm sure the store needed to get everyone moving to make some space for incoming customers.

Queenie won first prize and was given a crown. Ripper won title to the smallest prize. Dude won the coolest prize. Mickey and Minnie won the cutest couple prize. Greta won best dressed. Pinks won the ballerina title. Teel won big foot title. Annie won the scariest witch. Bear won most musical.

As Nurse Betty was to be named the most caring, the twins yelled out, "What is that smell?"

Everyone turned to see doo doo all around Nurse Betty's back legs, and there was a lot.

"I guess she did not do well with the bed pan lessons," Jay commented.

Nurse Betty's mother started to rush to the scene. I do not know whether one of the twins put his foot out or she slipped, but the result was the same. She landed right on top of Nurse Betty's business. Because of the momentum she was traveling at, she continued to slide right past us.

A customer opened the entrance door to come in just as she got near the door, and Nurse Betty's mom went sailing straight outside. Nurse Betty, true to her caring nature, galloped after Mom to rescue her.

From that point on everything became chaotic. Other customers were sliding and falling, all to the music of Bear's music grinder, which really was not the best tune for this. I believe it was "Tip Toe through the Tulips." In this case we had no tulips. Babes said this was better than a slip-and-slide, except for the brown stuff.

The store had called the paramedics for Nurse Betty's mom, who still had not reappeared. The manager was saying everyone needed to go outside so they could disinfect the store. That was certainly agreeable to all, because the smell was causing everyone to head toward the door on their own.

Upon hearing the sound of the sirens, I said, "We need to split."

Before getting into the love bug, the twins checked everyone's shoes. We again escaped just as the police and paramedics arrived.

I asked Steve if we could stop by the Fortune Cookie on the way home. "I have ordered dinner for everyone." That picked everyone's spirits up.

As we pulled in front of the restaurant, Jack said, "You will probably be a few minutes."

Little did we know I would be more than a few minutes.

CHAPTER 18

As soon as I entered the restaurant I was greeted by a waiter. I said, "I have an order to pick up. The name is Muldahl." I also had the stash hidden under my blouse.

"Your order is very large. Come with me to help carry all of it," he said.

I followed him behind the cash register and into a back room. As soon as I passed the entranceway, the door shut behind me, and my alarm signals went up. My hands were pulled behind my back and taped. Tape was placed over my mouth before I could scream. Next a bag was placed over my head, and I was hustled out to a van, or what felt like a van. Before closing the door, my feet were tapped also.

The next thing I knew we were moving and very fast. There was not much inside the van to keep me from rolling around. With each turn I went rolling from one side to the other, banging on the side panels.

Tears started to roll down my cheeks. I didn't think I would get out of this alive. No one knew where I was or were I was going. I still had the stash under my blouse, which was not a good thing. I wished Ripper was with me. I had told him to stay with Annie. The last I saw Rip he was sitting on top of Annie's witch hat. I thought of Borgs. I thought of Tom. I then said a prayer. I told myself, *Be brave. Think what you can do. Can you find a weapon to use?*

Becoming restless with the long wait, Jay and Steve decided to investigate. Everyone else decided to follow. The love bug door was not secured, and the animals followed as well, except for Teel. The step was too high for her.

Not seeing me, they demanded to know from the first waiter they saw were I was. He stated he knew nothing. Annie had moved forward and was sniffing the ground and followed it to the door behind the cash register. Greta was right behind her, and Ripper let out a screech.

Everyone ran for the door, pushing aside the waiter. Actually, they flattened him against the wall. Once the door was open, they found that there was no sign of me. The animals were all over the back room. Pinks was on her hind legs and twirling. Queenie had scratched open a big bag of rice that was spilling on the floor. Steve had grabbed another waiter by the shirt collar and threatened him, banging his head against the wall unless he told him were I was.

The shadow across the lot and under the trees noticed the commotion and signaled Tom. Borgs went flying out the back door with all the animals in hot pursuit. Dude swaggered. Everyone was slipping on the rice.

The church ladies had just returned from another service and saw all of this action as they pulled into the driveway to their apartment. They got hot on the phone to the police, saying, "There is a MacDonald's farm taking place at the Fortune Cookie."

The operator asked them to explain what they meant. They tried to calm down. "There is a short witch with a green bat sitting on top of its hat. Two pumpkins walking around on four paws each. A striped prison-looking cat with a top hat. A pink cat wearing a tutu. The lion king dressed in drag. A goose dressed like it belongs on the MacDonald farm, only with an attitude." They noticed that attitude also. "It is in charge mode. A lot of people are also running around yelling 'Inga.' Just a minute ago a white van went speeding out of there and almost hit us as we were trying to pull in. Right behind the van was a ghost. He stopped long enough to look at us and say 'Boo!' Behind the ghost is a big black dog that looks like a pony and is keeping up with the ghost."

The dispatcher, being a little devilish by nature (maybe related to the twins), asked, "Do you see any big black panthers?"

"Are you making fun of me?"

"A patrol car has already been sent. Enjoy the show!" Disconnect.

Then they heard the sirens and saw flashing lights.

Both Chief Bob and Tom rushed into the restaurant, trying to keep their balance with the rice on the floor. They found Borgs outside in the back of the restaurant.

Borgs was yelling, "Thank you, Tully!" She was pointing at the sky.

Written on the sky was a rectangle, and inside the rectangle were numbers and letters. Tom reached Borgs.

She grabbed his arm and said, "That's the plate of the van that has abducted Inga. Tully left it for us."

Tom turned to his brother and said, "Get a BOLO out on that tag. They are traveling north on interstate 95. They have maybe a fifteen-minute start on us. Let's call BSO and Ft. Lauderdale Police. Oh, don't forget to call Smokey."

Chief Bob said, "How do you know that is the plate? What about the plant you have on Inga?"

"Trust me, Bob, if Borgs said that is the plate, you can bet your last dollar on it. I have learned not to question these things. These girls have very high connections. Inga is wearing the bug, and we are tracking her. We need air coverage. I have my helicopter arriving any minute."

They heard the blades. It landed. Tom jumped aboard, and the helicopter was back in the air. After the shadow had called in the distress, he had also taken off in pursuit of the van. He was a little behind Tully. He called Tom and gave the coordinates of the van. Tom relayed them to Bob, and Bob called Ft. Lauderdale.

There was a blockade waiting on 95 and Griffin Road. The van had no place to go and stopped. Tom had his chopper land right on 95. The entire road was shut down. The Ft. Lauderdale Police had already pulled out the driver and passenger. They were cuffed and read their rights.

Tom flashed his ID to an officer close by and ran for the back of the van. He opened the door. He took a deep breath. There she was. Thank God. He jumped in and took off the bag. He removed the tape and held her as she cried uncontrollably in his arms.

By this time there were TV camera crews all over and in the air as well. Chief Bob had landed also in his chopper.

Tom yelled, "I'm taking her to the hospital! Please handle the questions! Call if you need me!"

"Okay, bro."

Tom picked up Inga and carried her to the waiting chopper.

The camera crews asked, "Who is the mystery man? He came in like Superman. That must be the heroine he is carrying."

The Channel 7 cameraman said, "We need to find out who the mystery man is. There he goes, folks. He is up, up, and away. Is it a plane? No, it is the mystery man."

They flew right to the Shores hospital. They were alerted and had a staff waiting. Tom called Borgs, and everyone loaded into the love bug and headed toward the hospital. That would be an interesting scene. E-I-E-I-O.

When the shadow filed his report much later, he never mentioned the ghost or Pony Dog. He was no fool.

They had to give Inga a tranquillizer so they could pry her fingers off Tom. She was very bruised and traumatized. Before long she was highly sedated and sleeping like a little angel.

CHAPTER 19

I was badly bruised, but they let me go home from the hospital in the afternoon of the next day. I was given pain pills and told I would not be able to be out of bed for very long without getting tired. I could see my body changing colors before my eyes. I was a walking rainbow.

We had planned our monthly dinner for that evening, and I did not want to miss it. Tom had said he would fix the salad and pick up all the paper goods. I did not have to worry about any preparations.

We normally had our dinner party on the roof. We had strung lights all around the perimeters of half the roof. A small refrigerator, sink, and grill were enclosed in an aluminum shed by the stairs. That left plenty of room for entertainment or dancing and enough tables and chairs for a sit-down meal. When this was not in use for parties, some of us used it for sunbathing. The other half of the roof was dedicated to a vegetable garden and Mama Rosa's orchids, which I understand Frank the plumber was working on.

We all enjoyed the fresh vegetables we produced, and most of us pitched in to keep the garden up. Mama Rosa had told me our guest list for the dinner was really growing. Three retired couples from the first floor were joining us. She said some tenants were still out of town. Also, Babes was bringing Officer Mendez, and Crane had invited Slim's son.

Slim's son also worked at the dad's restaurant on an as-needed bases. He had met Crane through Babes. Otherwise, he was pursuing a career in aviation. He was slim also like the dad and very tall. Mama had invited Frank, Frank's daughter Maria Jade, and Frank's son Tony, who I was told by Mama was very handsome, "perfect for Gina."

The okay sign was given from the propeller arms and a wink for good measure. Si. Borgs had called to say they were closing the Pie early so they could all join us. Tom said that his brother and the Shores mayor were going to stop by, along with Smokey. Yes, it was going to be quite a group. Mama kept making more lasagna.

Our table had Borgs, Chief Walter, Mayor Al Travis, Smokey, Tom, and myself. Cabby was standing behind my chair since he wanted to join the Pie crew for dinner but also wanted to hear what was being said at our table. Tom and I were holding hands under the table.

Tom began by saying that last evening had been a huge success. I reached up and squeezed Cabby's hand.

Tom said, "An envelope of pictures had been left on the scene at the restaurant that tied the van drivers to the drugs found in the linens, and this lead to their employer, who was the king pin for the northeast coast Chinese restaurant drug trafficking."

Smokey attested to this and said he needed to leave shortly to catch his plane to Washington. He would be in charge of handling the case on a national level, but he was not leaving until he had Mama Rosa's lasagna.

I then found out that Homey had been his employee and was a plant to be near the Chinese restaurant without creating suspicion. Unfortunately for him the cover was lost. Officer Mendez had been instructed to come out of the bathroom of Slims at the designated time that Homey was robbing the restaurant and shoot the gun out of Homey's hand.

Here Babes became involved and was also a heroine. Chief Bob had been alerted that trouble was on its way with big-time drugs by Tom, who was working on a case in Palm Beach that included a Chinese restaurant and drugs. When a permit was purchased to open a Chinese restaurant in the Shores and the permit carried the same owner's name as the Palm Beach restaurant, Tom called in the FBI.

Bob and Tom were also aware of my involvement and knew that Curious Georgi was not going to leave things alone. That was when I was given the fortune cookie necklace that was bugged. The Fortune Cookie's security camera had caught Cabby and me on film. So we had endangered ourselves.

Tom told me later that they had tracked the camera from the pictures left at the restaurant to a local spy store and then linked the credit card to Cabby. This was not mentioned, nor the identification of the big black panther that was seen at the restaurant and later entering the Pointe. Good thing Tom was not a blabbermouth.

They continued saying how the story had gone on the national news partly due to the police chase on 95 and the dramatic helicopter rescue. This is where Mayor Travis came in, and now I knew why he had been invited. They wanted to recognize the event by sending a warning to drug dealers in our area to stay out of the Shores. My picture had been matched to the one with the football interview, and the media wanted more coverage, and now United Airlines, who was identified by my uniform in the interview, wanted more coverage. I was the only one who didn't want more coverage. After all, I was a rainbow baby and needed to stay in bed.

What they proposed was a parade down the center of Miami Shores in honor of me. The media still had not identified the mystery man, and Tom wanted it to stay that way. They now all stopped talking, and everyone stared at me.

I thought, *Why did I want to get out of the hospital to come to this dinner?*

Borgs said she had spoken to my boss again, and my vacation was extended by two months. Tom squeezed my hand.

"I know it will take time to make these arrangements, so I don't think I need to give you an answer right now. How about a few days from now when I am feeling better?" I cleverly answered.

What could they say? Everyone agreed and smiled, because they knew I would be agreeing in a few days. They could afford to be patient. I was thinking I could get out of town in a few days, so I was smiling also.

Smokey had been served dinner early. Upon finishing he handed over a large bag, which he had stored under the table. He said that he did not want to come empty-handed. Inside were bags of fortune cookies for everyone. There were cheers and claps as he got up to go.

He stopped by my chair, shook my hand to thank me, and then leaned over and softly whispered, "I would catch you anytime."

I looked up into his face and could swear smoke was swirling around his head. He smiled and was gone.

Tom didn't miss a trick and said, "What was that about?"

"Is this necklace bugged for sound or GPS or both?" I asked.

"GPS only."

"Then I don't recall what was said." Tit for tat. I hadn't put a plant on his neck.

It was time for the feast. I was starved. There was plenty of food. We all cheered for Mama Rosa.

Jay and Steve had started playing songs on their guitars and invited Maria Jade to sing with them. Who knew she was so talented? I guess the twins did. She had a beautiful, clear, sweet tone. She was also professional in style, keeping up with hand gestures to match the words to the song. Maybe that is an Italian thing. We cheered and asked her to sing some more. Her last song was about a harvest, moon, and hayride. We all joined in.

Jay announced it was time for the long-awaited Chicken Dance. I was excused. Gina, Mama Rosa, Maria Jade, Babes, and Crane all got ready. I could see the twins winking at each other.

The music began, and when everyone squatted I heard a *toot toot*. I looked at Gina, and she was looking at Mama Rosa with an embarrassed expression. The twins were smirking, and Mama Rosa was tooting. Oh dear.

The beat was getting faster. Mama Rosa was using her propeller arms like great chicken wings, flapping up and down in between tooting. Gina and I started yelling and cheering every time we saw Mama start to bend.

The twins countered with a rubber chicken they had bought that when squeezed sounded like someone had let loose hot air. By this time everyone had enough wine and was giggling, if not outright laughing hysterically. Finally it came to an end. Excuse the word.

Mama was declared the Chicken Dance queen. They then placed a crown on her head that looked like the one that Queenie had gotten at the Halloween costume event. It was a small crown, but it did not matter. Mama beamed, and everyone took pictures, along with Frank. I noticed Tony had his arm around Gina, and she was not objecting. Then we heard that disgusting chicken noise. The twins announced the entertainment was over.

Borgs mentioned she had to help me down to bed. She told me on the way down that Tully was stopping by. Once inside the apartment, she went right to the window. I followed her. Looking out, we saw a ghost figure in front of a Miami moon. It was doing a happy dance. It also looked like it had a pumpkin in his hand.

We both said, "Tully that is not fair. You cannot go trick-or-treating."

We saw something coming our way. Once it landed, we picked it up and saw it was a dog treat. Now we understood.

"*You* are giving out the treats."

Tully did another happy dance, blew kisses, and flew off.

Once in bed, I waited for Tom. I was not disappointed. I got a lingering kiss that made the other one seem like grammar school. Wow. If I had socks on they would have shot off my feet. I felt like I was icing from a cake and melting. My heart was in Borg's aerobic class. A sigh cannot be a sigh if the kiss was not a kiss. I think I'm getting it.

"Could we try this again?" I sweetly asked.

Tom smiled and gently held me in his arms. Now a sigh was a sigh.

CHAPTER 20

I had spent several days in bed. I was still black and blue and had trouble walking, but Borgs suggested that we go forward with our GD incentive for the Pie employees. I agreed. Besides, the outing would do me good. There was no doubt who the winner was. We thought since the GD was so stupendous that we needed to do something stupendous in return. We decided we would take all the Pie staff out to join Cabby for lunch in his celebration. We selected Smith and Wollensky on South Point. They were known for their beef. Borgs made the reservation. She reminded me for the second time to wear something nice.

What did that mean? I wasn't planning on going in my pajamas. I had to wear something that covered most of the bruises. I didn't want to scare anyone, even if it was the season. I picked a long Jam World dress with a shawl for my shoulders and arms. The dress had beautiful colors of yellow, red, and green. Koi in orange and gold were swimming on the print. I wore some long mother-of-pearl earrings that were shaped like fish, and wore yellow wedge scandals.

Borgs drove me, and the Pie crew took the smart car minus the chef on top; after all, we were going to a classy restaurant.

Once inside, we were given a seat by the window. I had to be assisted with a wheelchair. We looked out onto Government Cut, watching passing boats and jet skis. People passed by on the sidewalk with roller blades and bikes or were just walking their dog. It was relaxing and very beautiful.

Once I was given a menu my stomach churned and said, "I'm hungry." Everyone else must have saved their appetite too, since we all agreed to order right away, and I was impressed, along with the waiter, with the banquet-size order.

While we waited Borgs announced our winner was Cabby. She then said that this was our first event, but also it was extremely special, so we decided everyone should celebrate along with the winner. We also picked a very special present for Cabby. We handed Cabby a gift certificate for five hundred dollars to Green Spot, which was our local bike store on Northeast 6th Avenue."

"Cabby, we know how much you enjoy bike riding and thought you could pick out the bike of your dreams with this."

Cabby was thrilled, and we took lots of pictures. Borgs kidded me about how they had to pry my fingers off Tom at the hospital. They only succeed once I was tranquilized.

"You don't let go of a good thing when you see it," I remarked.

Everyone laughed.

The food arrived, and all conversation stopped for at least ten minutes. Then it resumed for, "Please pass the hash browns," or "Please pass the mushrooms." The dish was passed, and all was quiet again.

After an hour, and close to bursting, we began to back off of the forced feeding. We decided to control ourselves with dessert and said since they were so large we could share. One of their specials was coconut cake. So we ordered one, then two, and finalized it with three. You only live once. Everyone agreed we had a great afternoon.

As we were leaving, Tom's Porsche pulled up. He got out and tossed the valet his keys and said, "Keep it up front," He then approached Borgs and me and told Borgs he would take over the wheelchair.

Borgs winked at me and said, "See you later."

Tom wheeled me down by the water. He lifted me out of the chair and set me on the rocks along the water's edge.

"I don't want to alarm you, but this is something I need to do, and it will not wait any longer."

I must admit, he had my interest.

He took a little box from his pocket and said, "I am not pressuring you. You can take all the time you want. I just want you to know how I feel."

He asked for my left hand. I was almost afraid to hand over my hand.

Tom opened the box and placed a chocolate one-carat emerald-cut diamond on my pinkie. "I am promising to be here for you whenever you want to make a commitment. You take your time. Make sure this is what you want. Tell me, and I will be there. I am ready to make that commitment whenever you are. I never want you to be unhappy again."

I let out my breath. How perfect. He was not forcing an engagement but promising only his commitment to me, allowing me to take my time and make that big decision when I was ready. I looked down at the ring he had placed on my finger. It was a bit large for a pinkie ring, but it did make a statement I could not ignore. I noticed little diamonds around the emerald cut. It was a perfect promise.

When I looked up, a waiter was approaching with a bucket of chilled champagne and a peach rose on the tray. Tom poured us drinks. We held them up to toast as a violin began to play our favorite song, "A World that Was Wonderful."

It was so beautiful. I looked out at the water; it was gorgeous. I looked at my ring; it was gorgeous. I looked up at Tom with tears in my eyes and said, "What took you so long?" And he was gorgeous.

CHAPTER 21

The mayor was busy making plans. The date selected for the parade was October 31st. Following the parade there would be a party for the Shores trick-or-treaters. The businesses in the Shores were busy with their plans of entertainment for the children and buying candy. My car was sent to Shores Auto Repair for JR to check everything over and make sure there would be no problems, since I was to be driven in this car.

They assumed I had agreed to the plan, and since I was still in town, I guess I had. I decided on wearing white slacks with a long-sleeve red, white, and blue shirt. It wasn't much in fall colors, but it was okay to be on the patriotic side. The media was ready.

In my car Cabby was driving. I had bought him a nice red baseball cap. Tom rode shotgun. In the back Chief Walters sat next to me, and Mayor Travis was on the other side. For once I didn't worry about how fast we were going.

We were at the end of the parade. Ripper was on the back of my neck and came out only when pictures were being taken. I held a peach rose. I couldn't remember the last time the Shores had a parade. Banners waving from streetlights stating: Drug-Free Shores. What a crowd had come for the celebration! How exciting it was.

Behind my convertible was the Pie delivery car, and the chef was in all his glory on top. Borgs wasn't missing a chance like this to advertise. She was also driving.

I heard the sound of hoofs before I turned, and I saw Bear galloping up Main Street with Miss Kelly on his back. They passed Borg's car and came alongside mine and just trotted along next to me. Kelly leaned over and said they couldn't miss the event. Bear was drooling, and Annie wasn't even around.

I heard a toot from the horn of the Pie car. I knew Borgs was signaling me. I was in trouble. Again. I ignored it. Again.

As we passed the police station Gina was busy taking pictures, and next to her was Betty Perfect. Betty Perfect called out and waved to Chief Bob, then the mayor, and of course Tom. There was no wave for me. I gritted my teeth and again asked forgiveness for my thoughts.

I heard Channel 7 in passing say, "Hey, that's the mystery man."

His cameraman said, "He looks like her bodyguard."

Just then Tom turned around and grabbed my hand and brought it to his lips.

The cameraman then said, "That's no bodyguard."

I noticed Betty Perfect watching, and I smiled at her. I looked down at my beautiful ring. After all, I could afford to be charitable. Really.